Roxanne

"In untwisting the strands of biology and intimacy that make up families, *Someone Else's Son* performs one of fiction's most serious tasks: to take up part of everyday life and reveal how dangerous, how necessary, and how deeply mysterious it is."

—James Lindemann Nelson
Associate for Ethical Studies, The Hastings Center

"*Someone Else's Son* raises issues that touch many lives . . . more so than simply those who ponder the possibility of 'switched' babies. While this book touches a 'timely' nerve, it is a nerve that, seemingly, was sensitive long before the age of genetic engineering. One cannot help but wonder about the newborn game played at hospital nursery windows—a theme continued throughout life and which intensifies during family reunions—'he has Uncle Joe's thumbs . . . Grandpa's ears . . . he walks like Aunt Mary . . . he has Papa's smile.' Why the constant fascination with identifying family traits? What reassurance do we seek for ourselves in this universal game? What, indeed!"

—Simone D. Zelner, Ph.D.
Psychologist

SOMEONE ELSE'S SON

ALAN A. WINTER

MASTERMEDIA LIMITED, New York

Copyright © 1993 Alan A. Winter

All rights reserved, including the right of reproduction in whole or in part, in any form.
Published by MasterMedia Limited.

MASTERMEDIA and colophon are registered trademarks of MasterMedia Limited.

Library of Congress Cataloging-in-Publication data

Winter, Alan A.
 Someone else's son / Alan Winter.
  p. cm.
 ISBN 0-942361-75-X (hard) : $18.95
 1. Infants switched at birth—United States—Fiction. 2. Parent and child—United States—Fiction. I. Title.
PS3573.I5367S65 1993
813'.54—dc20   *93-20134*
           CIP

Author's photo by Susan Johann
Manufactured in the United States of America

10 9 8 7 6 5 4 3 2 1

For my sons—
Scott, Jordan, and Ryan

FOREWORD

The iceberg has poked through the waters and the titanic problem of children searching for a biological parent is an ever-frequent event. One only need look at newspaper headlines or TV's magazine-like programs to bear witness to this phenomenon.

GRANDMOTHER GIVES BIRTH TO OWN
GRANDDAUGHTER

BABY M'S MOTHER SUES TO KEEP HER

SPERM MIX-UP: LONG ISLAND WOMAN
GETS WRONG SPERM—HAS BLACK CHILD

FERTILITY DOCTOR FATHERS 72 CHILDREN

Screaming headlines as these have become commonplace. What will the future bear as fertility experts help thousands of hopefuls have children? We know that single parents and couples wanting to raise a child go to extremes to accomplish their goal. These long-awaited births bring instant joy. But for these parents, for scientists, fertility experts, and religious leaders, all living in a society accustomed to the means justifying the ends, questions arise that need answers.

The reality is this: Scores of children will not be genetically related to one or both parents.

Surrogate mothers, anonymous sperm donors, in vitro mixing of a stranger's sperm with a would-be father's low count, all serve to increase the chances of fertilization. A short time ago, these advances didn't exist, now they are everyday procedures. This new frontier, plus an isolated error here or there, create the potential for a chromosomal nightmare. One day, too, the children born out of this biological revolution will grapple with the question of whose genes are in their blood. Some will shrug a shoulder, while others will search for a parent with matching DNA. Worse yet, the possibility exists that genetically related siblings, children created by one of these new technologies and living with different families, will meet and marry.

Last year, Dan Quayle set off a rage of comments when he used the popular television character, Murphy Brown, as an example of our country's declining moral values. But the issue is who are the real parents. Since 1984, state agencies have been required to help parents collect child support payments, and of the 12 million cases currently handled, only 18 percent receive money. Some states mandate that parents be responsible for their offspring, not the local government. As a result, tens of thousands of men are tested annually in DNA labs across the country. If proven to be the rightful parents of a state-supported child, their wages are garnished. Along the way, mistakes are noted, and some men who think they are a child's father find out they're not. Think of the havoc.

The same exists in some divorce cases. A friend tells the story of a man trying to limit the distance his estranged wife be allowed to take their fifteen-year-old. When negotiations reached an impasse, the mother coolly stated it was a moot point, the child was not his. The man had no idea he had raised another man's son, and now he had to deal with what, if any, were his parental rights. Was he legally the father? Was he duty-bound to pay child support? Could the mother take the child across state lines? This is not an isolated case.

Not only can science help infertile couples, but DNA fingerprinting can tell who belongs to whom. Each person in the world, except for identical twins, has a unique genetic code found in all body tissues, and is most commonly analyzed through hair, semen, and blood samples. This technology is used in custody cases, inheritance disputes, forensic criminal investigations, and identifications in times of war and disasters. Under proper laboratory conditions, DNA testing is definitive.

A last issue remains.

Haven't you ever heard a parent say, "I don't know where you came from. You *can't* be my child." Everyone has heard a sibling tease another saying, "You're not my sister, you're adopted." Are these idle threats or real fears?

At one time or another, most of us have stared into a mirror, touched our lips, felt our noses, wrinkled our brows, and checked our smiles to see if they were similar to a parent's or sibling's. It is human nature to question our origin. What would you do if this sense of insecurity, this irrational feeling were real?

We all know that in delivery rooms and birthing suites, newborns have their family names banded to their wrists and have their footprints recorded. In some hospitals, a mother's fingerprints are also taken. Yet the only check to see if a mother leaves with the right child is comparing wristbands for matching names. Was her child's identification tag temporarily removed for some reason or another? Was it removed to insert an IV? Nurses have reported tags found on the floor, and that some slip off at bath time.

Are mistakes made? Are babies switched? Have mothers brought home the wrong child?

It has happened.

Once the mistake has been discovered, it is often too late to do anything about it. How should it be handled? More importantly, what has the greater influence on a child: environment or genes?

Someone Else's Son explores this very haunting possibility in the story of Phillip Hunter. His story opens many questions for all those who are on a quest to unravel the unsolved mystery of who they are.

Alan A. Winter
New York, 1993

SOMEONE ELSE'S SON

1

❧❧

The sudden afternoon storm caught nearly everyone by surprise, everyone that is, except Frank Bellman. His bones warned him long before the angry clouds rolled in from the west, long before others had time to seek shelter or wished they weren't mired in late afternoon traffic jams. He didn't notice the large drops that splashed on his windshield or the steam rising from the hood of his gray Honda Accord. It had been a particularly dry summer and the hardened ground could not absorb the rainwater that ran off in muddied rivulets. Besides warning him of the barometric change, his bones also told him not to get out of his car, not to ring the doorbell, not to raise their suspicions.

Not heeding his intuition, he did ring the buzzer.

"Frank, where's your umbrella?" asked Brad Hunter.

Rain splattered off Frank's bald head. It gushed down his cheeks, gathered along his slack chin and plopped onto his forest green suede loafers.

"I . . . uh . . ."

"Don't just stand there. Come in." Brad Hunter, who was a couple of years younger and taller, ushered his brother-in-law in out of the rain. "Must've been a bitch

1

driving here. Is Walnut Street flooded? Usually is." Brad took Frank's rumpled tan raincoat as Frank wiped his face with a handkerchief.

"Want a drink?"

"Do I ever need one! Scotch—straight up."

"Which album is that?" Brad asked, placing the drink on the polished coffee table. Frank was busy turning the pages of a family photo album he'd casually picked from the middle shelf of the cherry wood bookcase in the living room.

"Dunno. Guess I never saw this one before." He pointed to a boy crouched in a powder blue Little League uniform, eyes fixed on an unseen ball. "Is that Phillip?"

"Ummmm, I can't . . . uh . . . speaking of Phillip, how's he doing at the lab?"

"Great! He never stops asking questions—wants to know how every experiment works and why we're doing them. Between all his chattering, though, he cleans the animal cages and keeps the lab in order. He's something else."

Brad reached into his pocket. "Shit, I left my glasses upstairs. This middle-age business sucks. Nothing's the same anymore."

"Look who's talking. You're still at a good fighting weight. Bet you weigh the same as when you graduated college. Look at me," Frank grabbed a handful of his ample midsection. "And you have your hair, you bastard. What're you complaining about?"

Frank looked like Friar Tuck while Brad resembled a trim, muscular Robin Hood. Brad's nostrils were narrow and his lips were a bit thin. His honey-brown eyebrows were bushy and he had a slightly raised mole on his left cheek that could only be seen from the side. Though the individual features were unspectacular, even flawed, the total package produced a man that turned heads.

Brad leaned closer.

"Lemme see," he said, "most of the time, the kids' pictures look the same to me."

He put the photo at arm's length and then slowly brought it forward, squinting.

"Nope, that's Todd—hair's straight. Phillip's hair was always wavy. Ron, on the other hand, had brown hair from the time he was born. I have no idea who he takes after. He's the only one with dark hair in the family."

"Of course, it's Todd. I should've realized it, Phillip's a lefty."

"With most things, Frank, but he bats righty."

Brad studied his brother-in-law, noting how he lingered over the pictures, then flipped the pages only to return to one he'd already seen. Brad was about to ask if anything was wrong when Frank closed the book and downed the rest of his drink.

"Great looking boys, Brad. You and Trish are mighty lucky."

"Hey, the boys have a great looking mother. And you're right, we are plenty proud of them."

Flakes of the white cocktail napkin trickled from Frank's meaty hand. His bloodshot eyes bulged as he struggled to dislodge the prickly air stuck in his throat.

"Brad, sorry to barge in this way but Myrna's ready to throw the steam shower out; it's been sitting on our bathroom floor for six months. I haven't had time to put it in."

"Christ, when Myrna makes up her mind, nothing stops her. Is that why you're here?"

"It was today or never. I needed to see the connections. D'you mind?"

Brad grinned. "Sure thing. I bet you're sorry you got married again?"

"Not on your life. Marrying Myrna was the best thing I ever did. It was hard raising Kevin without a mother. Christ, it was

3

the longest eight years of my life. I never knew if I was supposed to be his disciplinarian or his buddy. I did the best I could."

"I wouldn't have wanted to switch places with you."

"No," he said, wagging his head, "men aren't cut out for raising kids alone." Then he sat back and his chest swelled, reinflated by Myrna's image. "These last two years have given me a new life."

"It must've been tough when your wife died."

Frank slumped. "Hey, I'd better check those fittings and get out of here. My bride's waiting, you know."

"Want a hand?"

"No, thanks. It'll just take a minute. I know where it is." Before Brad could offer again, Frank climbed the stairs, pulling on the wrought iron rail so he could make the top step. He waited to catch his breath, promising himself to begin a diet that night.

He opened the linen closet that housed the steam-heating unit and knocked and clanged the connectors. He rattled the copper pipes and then deftly slipped into the master bathroom, pulling open the vanity drawer next to the sink. Taking what he came after, he slipped the envelope in his breast pocket and returned to the hall area. Satisfied with his performance, Frank poked his head in the kitchen where Brad prepared dinner the one night his wife worked late.

The next morning, Phillip Hunter took a parking space well away from careless drivers who had damaged his 4.0 litre red Jeep Cherokee. The day before, he had found a scratch and had vowed he would never again park in a tight space. With long, muscular legs, the sinewy eighteen-year-old strode across the parking lot. He would be studying veterinary medicine in the fall at Cornell and was lucky his aunt had

4

recently married a researcher who worked with animals: Uncle Frank.

Parker Pharmaceuticals, no different from any of the other large steel and glass structures dotting Route 287 in western New Jersey, had windows like one-way mirrors: those inside could see out but no one could see in. A hundred eyes could be staring at him and he would never know. Phillip had the same feeling when in the company of people who wore reflective sunglasses. "Keep your distance," was their message, "no one is permitted to see what lies on the other side." Did the research laboratory harbor any secrets?

It was Phillip's third day on his summer job. The portly security guard with the shoulder-length hair escaping from the sides of his cap, flashed his Cheshire-white greeting. "Buenas Dias!" Phillip returned the salute. Phillip found his locker; he had requested number 111 so he could remember it easily. Numbers still confused him. He pulled out the freshly bleached lab coat that hung on a metal hook. He needed to pry the arms open because too much starch had been used. Stiffly, à la Frankenstein, he lurched to his uncle's lab and attacked his chores.

He cleaned each cage, arranging them on the counter top in a straight line. Spotting a plumed handle under a sink, he feather dusted the cage tops. If glassware was dirty, he washed it. If supplies needed to be put away, he found their correct places. Time slipped by unnoticed until Phillip heard a commotion. Two delivery men were trying to maneuver an over-sized crate on an under-sized dolly through the lab door.

"No! No! No!" Frank pleaded. "Take the door off its hinges. That will give you enough room, gentlemen."

"Hey, Doc, leave this to the professionals. We'll get the job done," one of them said.

5

"That's what I'm afraid of." Frank returned to his office muttering, "Where do they find these jerks?" Once the laboratory director was gone, the struggle continued until the delivery men yielded to Newton's Unalterable Law: any mass, no matter what its size, only fits through openings larger than itself. They submitted and removed the heavy metal door from its hinges.

Phillip watched in fascination. One wore a red scarf as a bandana and a matching strip that gathered his brown mane into a ponytail. Dark sunglasses as opaque and reflective as the building's windows, and six gold earrings through his left ear completed the look.

His partner had a large handlebar moustache and his shaven head glistened with sweat. Arms with swollen Popeye-like muscles bulged as he strained with the wooden container. One biceps sported a tattoo of Medusa surrounding the American flag while the other had a ring of hearts encircling an eagle with BE WILD—BE FREE written above it. The men wore matching navy blue pants and tee shirts. A pack of cigarettes was tucked in their sleeves, which were rolled up to their armpits. Emblazened across their shirts was the company's motto: YOU GOT IT, WE'LL SCHLEPP IT.

While the delivery men unpacked Frank's newly prized possession, an electron microscope, Phillip walked behind Mr. Soo into the room. Mr. Soo had been an oncologist in his native Korea. Unable to get a medical license in the States, he became a laboratory technician. Though slight of frame, he lifted large boxes with ease, clearing the area where the microscope would be installed. Together, they removed cartons filled with reports and computer printouts from old experiments. Phillip put the last box down and wondered how long they would remain untouched in their new site.

By early afternoon, the frantic energy of the morning

yielded to the more familiar pace of plain hectic. Drinking glass after glass of tap water, Frank informed them that the manufacturer would be sending a technician to calibrate the delicate instrument the next day. He breathed heavily. His cheeks, quivering masses of purple, pulsed.

"Tough morning, eh, Phillip?"

"It was okay, Uncle Frank." He grinned.

"What's so funny?"

"Oh, nothing."

"Something must be funny, you're smirking from ear-to-ear."

"The way you're sweating, it's a good thing you're in research."

"Wise ass!" Frank slapped him on his back and returned to his office. Phillip spent the rest of the afternoon stocking the animal cages with fresh provisions and putting away the assorted supplies the lab received daily. Finished, he walked into his uncle's office to say good-bye.

Frank peered through the ocular of a Zeiss-Nikon light microscope. When he heard someone at the door, he reflexively shut the light illuminating the glass slide.

"What're you doing?" Phillip asked.

"Nothing much. Why'd you ask?"

"Looked like you were doing the same thing we did yesterday, that's all."

"Actually, I'm checking data from an old experiment. Who knows how much longer I'll use this 'scope now that the new one's here?"

"Well, I finished everything."

"Thanks for your help, Phillip. Have fun tonight," he called.

"I will. I'm seeing Gillian after dinner."

Frank had met Phillip's girlfriend at their high school grad-

7

uation the previous week. They were both classmates of his son, Kevin, who was not going to college as they were, but worked as an auto mechanic.

Phillip took two steps and wheeled. "Say, isn't this your tennis night?"

"It's more like comedy night. It makes Myrna happy. When we got married, I promised we'd do things together. She took up tennis so I'm her amusement."

"Well, good luck," said Phillip.

On another evening, Frank might have chatted longer but he was disturbed by what he had just seen. Reluctantly, he turned the light under the slide on again and adjusted the fine tuning knob. He squinted through the small opening. "It can't be," echoed in the empty lab. Frank reached for the reference book hidden on the top shelf and compared what he saw to the pictures on the open page. His heart sank.

Frank left the lab to meet Myrna. Though fifteen minutes late, he made no effort to hustle. The stale air of the men's locker room was particularly evident that evening. Mindlessly, he twirled the tennis racket. The practice basket of yellow balls was nearly empty. Scattered yellow spheres littered the other side of the court like dandelions.

"I was beginning to think you'd forgotten. Anything wrong?" Frank didn't answer. He had married Trish Hunter's older sister and now stared at her high cheek bones and long face. It was as if he were looking at her for the first time. There were strong genes in that family. Myrna and Trish had the same-turned up nose, full lips and high forehead leading to silky straight hair. The touch of Myrna's lips on his cheek jarred him back to reality.

"Oh, I'm sorry. I was a thousand miles away. What'd you say, dear?" This time, he paid attention. "Nothing's wrong. The electron microscope arrived today and we worked like dogs getting it ready for tomorrow's installation. We couldn't have done it without Phillip." Then his mind flitted to what he had seen through the microscope.

"That's great!" She picked up the metal basket that retrieved the scattered tennis balls. "Let's volley and get a set in before we run out of time." In seconds, Myrna had cleared the court and hit a ball to Frank. It flew by him.

"Hey, Bellman, get with it!"

"Sorry," he said.

She hit another and he missed it.

"This counts. First serve in."

Settling down, Frank managed to make contact, though balls frequently sailed over Myrna's head or were trapped in the net. He lost 6–4, which made Myrna sense something was really wrong—she had never taken six games in an evening let alone win a set.

"Bellman! I won a set and not a word from you! Are you ill?" She looked at him suspiciously. Frank was staring at an empty court. He squared and looked at her.

"Myrna, what's your blood type?"

"My what?" She shook the racket menacingly. "Hey, no excuses. Admit it, I beat you for the first time so take it like a man. Don't change the subject."

"Your blood type. You know: A . . . B . . . O. Your blood type?"

"Is that the come-on line of the '90s? Something like, what's your astrological sign, baby? What gives? Uh oh, you're having one of those scientific trances."

Frank was unfazed. "It occurred to me I don't know your blood type. Shouldn't I, in case of an emergency?"

"Uh, I guess so," she faltered. "It's O."

Trish Hunter carried two plastic bags filled with last minute groceries along with a bag of Clinique products, a new bathing suit and a shift she had bought on sale during her

9

lunch break. Putting the food away she cringed each time the ceiling yelped when Todd, her youngest, dropped the free weights that were part of his summer's bulk-up program. His football coach expected twenty more pounds of muscle when he reported to football practice at the end of August. Trish put water in a pot to boil. Then, taking the stairs by twos, she tried on her new bathing suit, which had more holes than Swiss cheese. Black with lightning bolts of tangerine and frosty mint, it was perfect for the south of Portugal where she and Brad would soon be going, along with their friends, Rick and Susan Sturnweiss.

Trish worked hard at maintaining her former flight attendant's figure. At five-foot nine and thin-waisted with a short torso on deliciously long legs, she was never one to feel ignored when men were around. She removed her blouse and studied herself. Her breasts were pear-shaped, her smooth skin gently sloped to two pink nipples the size of half-dollars firmly pointing straight ahead. In spite of three children and getting past forty, her hips were narrow and her breasts defied gravity.

Out of the open window, she heard Brad yell to Ron as he pulled into the driveway. "Don't you ever give up?"

"Never, Dad. I've taken a hundred and fifteen shots from this spot alone. Maybe I'll have one more growth spurt and switch from baseball to basketball. Maybe a scout'll drive down the street and discover me. Maybe. . . ."

Ron was never at a loss for words. Brad used to say that Ron's obstetrician vaccinated him with a phonograph needle.

"Maybe what? Maybe my aunt'll grow testicles and become my uncle," Brad shouted back. He got out of his mustard-colored Volvo 240DL and walked toward his son. "No one will ever accuse you of being lazy. How 'bout giving me a shot?"

"Oh no, ladies and gentlemen! It's the old 'how about giving the dad a shot' shot." Ron rifled the ball to Brad. "How come fathers have to take a shot when their sons are playing basketball?"

"It's really quite simple, my dear boy. There's an unwritten rule that says fathers are never old until they stop playing ball with their sons or, worse yet, their sons beat them in basketball. Of course . . . " Brad twirled the ball in his palms, ". . . that day hasn't come yet."

With that, Brad kicked his right leg in the air, springing off his left foot. He used his left arm for balance and extended his right arm straight from the shoulder and lofted the ball in an arc over his head. His back was partially facing the basket. A "sky" hook. He hit what one sports announcer would describe as "just string, no iron!"

"Swish! Evvvvery time! How the hell do you do it? It's such a ridiculous shot." Ron stood there, his mouth open.

"Call it luck. I call it skill." Brad entered the garage breathing a sigh of relief and shook his head yet another time. He believed in the Divine Right of the Hoop, that heavenly intervention that helped fathers make shots they had no right attempting. How much longer would the god of Larry Bird and Magic Johnson be on his side?

With one foot inside the house, and Ron still agape, Brad heard Phillip honk his horn and turn into the driveway. He slapped his younger brother "five" as he drove by in the Jeep.

"Hey, Phillip. Don't get stuck playing ball with Bob Cousy, Jr. over there," Brad said. He pranced to hug Phillip. "Phew. You better shower before your mother smells you. Dinner will be ready soon."

Minutes later, Trish rang the bronze cow bell she and Brad had brought back from Switzerland. The trip was for their fifth anniversary; she never dreamt she would use the corny memento Brad insisted on buying. Having clanged the bell, Trish retreated before the trampling Hunter horde. Every night, in affirmation of Pavlov's famous experiment, her sons salivated at the blast of the cow bell and let nothing stand between them and the food.

Phillip was last to take a seat. Beads of water ran down his face. He never dried his hair, tied his sneaker laces, or fastened his belt.

Trish placed the hot dishes on trivets and everyone helped themselves. Mounds of spaghetti, stacks of sauce-drenched meatballs, and piles of salad and homemade garlic bread vanished.

"How's it going at the lab?" Brad asked.

"Great! Soo taught me how to use a microtome today."

"What's that?" Todd asked, a string of pasta dangling over his chin. With one slurp it was gone.

"Well, it's this machine, kind of like a deli slicer."

"Yeah, and what'd you do with it?" Todd asked, now a piece of garlic bread half sticking out of his mouth.

"It makes super-thin slices of the specimen."

"What kind of specimen, Phil? Dead people?" Ron poked Todd in the ribs.

"Hey, cut it out!"

"No, dead mice, stupid."

Trish wrinkled her nose.

Phillip continued. "We place the sliced section on a slide and study it under the microscope." By the time Phillip completed his account, everyone had licked their plates clean and he had yet to take a bite!

"May I be excused?" Ron asked.

"Me too," said Todd. The white contoured chair screeched against the tiled floor.

"Todd, how many times do I have to tell you to lift the chair? You know it leaves marks."

"I'll clean it."

"Like the last time?"

Todd slinked across the floor.

"Not so fast." Trish pointed to the dishwasher.

"I'll do it for you, Mom." Then Ron turned to Todd. "Watch this, little brother, so you do it right." He squirted lemon-scented Joy onto the plate and sponged it, knowing Trish liked to hear it squeal. Ron loaded the dishwasher.

"Anything else you want me to do? I just love helping my mother."

"Ron, you can cut the crap. Go relax," she said.

While Trish brewed chamomile, the boys went about their business. Phillip left to see his girlfriend while Ron watched television. Ron was a Yankee booster surrounded by a family of Mets fanatics. Brad insisted Ron rooted for the Yanks so he could be different—it was his way of getting attention.

Todd walked into the den without saying a word. He ignored the TV. He wouldn't have heard it with his headphones on anyway, his cassette blasting Eric Clapton's "Journeyman" tape. He sat on the couch reading Frank Herbert's *Heretics of the Planet Dune*. Brad stuck his head in, telling them he and Trish were taking a walk. Neither boy looked up.

Brad and Trish passed split level and colonial homes, each on a quarter of an acre of fertile soil that once belonged to a family named Barnett. They were the last of the six farming families whose land made up Livingston, New Jersey, when it was incorporated in 1813. Now the town was like any of the suburban bedroom communities in America, this one being eleven miles from Newark and twenty-eight from New York City.

They walked in silence for a while.

"Doesn't seem like Phillip's having any problems at the lab," Trish said.

"Nope. I spoke to Frank yesterday. He said he didn't see any."

"Do you remember the first time he wrote your name? You thought he was making fun of you. He was only six."

Brad kicked a rock.

"How was I supposed to know reversing the d's and b's was normal?"

"If only it were in his case," Trish whistled, "it would've made our lives so much simpler. Give the boy credit. He's overcome quite a handicap."

"Einstein had it."

"So did Thomas Edison and Leonardo da Vinci. We were fortunate his teachers picked up on the dyslexia early on. Do you remember all those drills and flash cards they had us do with him?"

"I sure do. It was obviously worth it." Brad strutted. "Einstein, Edison, da Vinci, and Hunter—now that's a group!"

"Don't get carried away. Phillip Hunter's in that group, not you."

"I can dream, can't I?"

Phillip darted up the walkway, tripping on one of those free weekly newspaper that appear at odd hours wrapped in misprinted white bread sleeves.

"Hi, Mrs. Davis, Gillian home?"

"Yes, she is, Phillip. Please come in and I'll tell her you're here." As she spoke, Phillip heard Gillian scurrying from the bathroom. There was no doubt she had been combing her long blond hair one last time.

The sun had not set but the Davis house was dark. His eyes followed Gillian's mother as she walked up the stairs. She wore a print dress with large flowers embroidered on it, mid-calf in length. It hung loosely and her trim figure was lost in it. Her hair was pulled back into a tight bun, held in place by a tortoise shell comb.

The living room was sparsely furnished. A thin blue rug, faded from use, occupied its center. A maple-stained console rested in front of a short couch and served as a coffee table. Rarely lit frosted hurricane lamps, with white hobnailed glass shades, sat on matching end tables, providing the only light. The spartan surroundings were reflections of how Mrs. Davis viewed life—before and after her husband died.

Phillip's thoughts were interrupted by Gillian loping down the stairs. She was wearing a hot pink shirt knotted at the waist with a picture of Madonna on it. Her mother trailed and didn't see the wink Gillian gave him.

"Mom, we'll be in the basement," she said and took Phillip's hand, missing a disapproving stare.

They walked down the narrow stairs. Phillip tilted his head so as not to bump into the low, inclined ceiling that Gillian's father had installed many years earlier. Reaching the bottom, Phillip instinctively ducked, though the acoustic tiles were deceptively three inches above his head.

Once out of sight, he spun Gillian and kissed her.

"Hey, what was that for?"

"I missed you."

"What if she comes down?"

"Relax, Gilly. The last time she tried that we weren't doing anything."

"It makes me nervous knowing she could barge in at any minute." Gillian scratched her arms. "I'm getting hives thinking about it."

"Get real. She's not coming down here." He tried to be reassuring but had his doubts about Mrs. Davis, too.

Sitting on a couch with the radio playing softly, they kept

15

an attentive ear. With his arm around her shoulder, Phillip pulled her toward him. Her head automatically tilted toward his, her lips parted. He looked to see if her eyes were open, but they were closed. He noticed she had used robin's egg eye-shadow for the first time.

They kissed and kissed. Phillip's hands moved over her back and arms. Without breaking for air, he untied the knot and reached under her shirt, almost grabbing her breast when the predictable Mrs. Davis could be heard pacing above. Gillian scrambled away from him. Frantic fingers tucked loose strands of hair behind her ear before fixing her shirt.

She cleared her throat. "So how was work today? Do you still like it?"

On cue, he raised his voice: "I like it a lot. You should have seen these two characters who delivered an electron microscope today. They insisted on forcing a large crate through a door that was obviously too small."

"So how did they finally do it?" she asked, staring into his eyes, smiling.

"Well, they made like they knew what they were doing and disregarded Frank's suggestion of taking the lab door off its hinges. When he left, that's exactly what they did."

"Did you see it work?"

"Not yet. A special technician's calibrating it tomorrow. Soo told me he'd let me try it sometime. You know the guy never stops working."

"Who?"

"Frank. Tonight I was ready to leave and he was still at it, looking through the light microscope."

"You have to respect that kind of dedication, Phillip. My father always told me the world was filled with doers and people waiting to have it done for them. It's the doers that get ahead in life."

16

"Look where it got your father. Do you miss him?"

A discarded rag doll, she sat contorted, her legs and arms limply about the couch.

"I think about him every day, some days more than others. When it gets real bad or I get scared, I sneak into her room and open this one drawer. It's filled with his shirts and sweaters. I bury my head in it, close my eyes and I take the deepest breath." Gillian's eyes fluttered shut. "And then I smell him, like he's still here. I press the clothes to my face and for a moment, I forget he's gone."

She wormed her way under his arm, her open hand inching into his chest.

"God, it must be rough losing a parent."

"You don't know how lucky you are."

2

❧❧

B rad tried to modulate his voice. It might have been the way Sid Bergen said, "Hello," or commented on the weather, but he knew the salesman was up to something . . . and that something wasn't in Brad's best interest.

"Listen, Sid, I don't give a rat's ass what your problems are. A deal's a deal."

"C'mon, Brad." Sid Bergen cleared his throat. "Don't be like that. I swear it's different this time. How long we know each other? Twenty-five? No, thirty years. In all that time, did I ever do you wrong?"

"Nice try, Sid. The question is: When did you ever do me right? You nickel and dimed me every chance you got. In the. . . ."

"But, Brad. . . ."

"Let me finish. In the old days, you didn't give a shit about me. You went after the big boys; I was small potatoes, then. But now I'm your biggest customer. You should've sprung for the metal futures, guaranteed your costs, 'cause you gotta make good on my prices."

"Bradley. Bradley." Sid crooned Brad's name. "What do I

have to do to convince you I can't deliver? I'll be eaten alive."
Visualizing Sid thrown into a tankful of piranhas appealed to
Brad. He held the phone away from his ear, avoiding Sid's
whining.

Brad recalled the first time he saw Sid walk into his father's
store nearly thirty years earlier. CeramiElectric Mold Company was not housed in a state-of-the-art facility then, but in
an old three-floor walk-up that had once been a speakeasy.
Brad could still see the ornate tin ceilings and the pass-
through window on the third floor, similar to a bank teller's
gate. He imagined messages passed under the brass grill
saying, "Dutch sent me," or, "I'm a friend of Louie," and
behind the reinforced door were jaunty-dressed men with
breezy women on their arms. Glasses filled with contraband
booze sloshed in crystal glasses as the molls shrieked every
time their "guy" won a bet at the illegal crap table.

One day, Brad's father introduced him to Sid Bergen, the
brass socket salesman. Both men were forty-two, but Sid
looked older because of his premature gray hair. Sid was a
big man, six-two and at least 250 pounds. He was a magna
cum laude graduate of the "School of Hard Knocks" and
never gave anyone a break unless he had to, and then only
grudgingly. In the end, everyone knew Sid Bergen got the
best of every deal. Rough at the edges, a two-fisted bastard
who would con his own mother, he knew how to get to
Brad's soft spot. But that was before.

"Sid. There's only one thing you can do for me. . . ."

"Name it, Brad, it's yours," Sid said.

"Deliver my fucking goods. I want my goddamned sockets. You should've paid for my merchandise when I gave
you the money instead of stretching the float. Face it, you got
caught with your pants down."

"Caught with my pants down? I might as well drop

my drawers in Macy's window. Let everybody see what you're doing to me. Your father would never've treated me this way."

Brad squeezed the plastic receiver so hard it creaked.

"It's bastards like you that put my father in an early grave. The poor schnook pleased everyone, fell for every salesmen's hard luck story. He bought crap he never needed and got stuck with plenty of shit. Trouble is, salesmen never saw him chug bottles of Maalox after they wrenched his guts."

"Your father was a gentleman," Sid said.

"He was a sucker. Send me my fucking goods."

Brad slammed the phone. Sid would deliver—he always did. Victories over salesmen were few and far between and Brad savored this one.

His time for gloating lasted less than a minute.

"Mr. Hunter, the printer is on line three," Katie said. Katie Nordstrom had been Brad's secretary for three years. She had corn-silk blond hair cropped to her ears and innocent blue eyes. Yet when she left work, she shed her mid-western skin for a black belt in Tai Kwon Do, giving private lessons to women who no longer wanted to be called defenseless.

"Hello, Joe."

"Hello, Mr. Hunter." Joe Campognini spoke softly. Something was wrong.

"What's up, Joe? The catalogues ready?"

"Well . . . that's why I'm calling, Mr. Hunter. There seems to be a small hitch." Joe tripped over the words.

Brad rolled his eyes and looked at the ceiling, saying to himself, "Here we go again. Battle stations! Battle stations! Enemy sub sighted at two o'clock. Submerge! Submerge!" What did he have to do for things to run smoothly? The pencil point snapped on the desk blotter.

"How small a hitch, Joe?"

"It's the color separator. His eyes have been bothering

him. He needs a vacation before your job. There's nothing I can do about it."

"That's not true, Joe. Tell him to take his vacation *after* he does my job. With the money he'll be making, he'll enjoy his vacation a lot more."

The pencil broke in half.

"I can't do that, Mr. Hunter." Brad looked at the receiver in disbelief. After fifteen years, Joe still didn't understand that timing was everything in the mail-order business.

"If that's what you think, pack up my stuff. I'll send a man first thing in the morning to get it. Is that okay, Joe?"

"But, Mr. Hunter? I was counting on that job. I've always made your catalogues!"

"In the past, Joe, you made good on your promises. You said August first. Can you deliver?" Brad no longer had patience with people forgetting what made their businesses successful in the first place: service.

"I'll do my best, Mr. Hunter."

"Your best isn't good enough. What's it going to be, Joe? I need them August first," he growled into the phone.

"You got it, Mr. Hunter. You'll have them on the first."

"Good. I expect to see the galleys by next week."

Having disposed of a potential problem, he hung up without saying good-bye. It was another normal day.

The phone rang where Trish worked.

"Radiology office. How may I. . . ."

"Do you have time for lunch?" asked Susan Sturnweiss. Susan was Trish's best friend.

"Give me five minutes."

They met at the nearby diner and, after a brief wait, were seated.

"Trish, are you ordering a cheese burger and fries?"

"And a chocolate malt," she said through her fingers, as if

muffling the words wouldn't trigger Susan.

Susan ducked under the table.

"Where do you hide it? You eat like a truck driver. It's not fair."

"Good genes. My mother was the same way."

After the waitress took their order, Trish asked, "Have you talked with Tabby Marksman? Seems she and Skip are trying for another."

"Aren't four kids enough? Besides, her youngest should start high school soon. She's home free," said Susan.

"Not according to her. She can't stand the thought of not having a child around. I think it's an escape from dealing with reality."

"Didn't you tell her changing diapers is a reality?"

"But that's not the best part. Skip has a low sperm count so they're thinking about a donor. The doctor says Tabby's not the problem."

Susan grabbed the table.

"Excuse me? Shooting blanks after four kids? Run this by me again."

"It's got something to do with a varicocele making the temperature too hot, or something like that. Tabby told me Skip's been wearing special underwear fitted with a pump to circulate cool water, but it hasn't helped."

"That's a turn-on. No wonder they can't conceive," Susan said.

"Forget that, would you use a donor?"

"I wouldn't have five children."

"Well, let's say you didn't have children?" prodded Trish.

"Ugh, you'd never know what problems you'd be getting. There are so many things that could go wrong."

"But that's true even with your own husband. If you ask me. . . ."

Susan grabbed Trish's hand.

"It's Vivian Gersten. She's with that ophthalmologist, Dr. Leitner."

Trish stole a glimpse.

"So that's what she meant."

"Meant what?"

"Well . . . ," Trish hesitated, not wanting to betray a confidence, "her husband's always performing surgery or making hospital rounds. A real workaholic. The man's like a shark; he needs to be moving constantly or he's dead in the water. Vivian says he sleeps every chance he gets. Hasn't touched her in months."

"Why should she be different? Once they turn forty, men's libidos get registered on the endangered species list."

Trish frowned.

"I'm serious," said Susan, "tell me I'm wrong."

"That's the trouble—you're right." Her chest sagged. "At least we don't have to worry where our husbands have been. The thought of. . . ."

"Trish, get real. Look at Vivian, she's fused to the chair. I love it. I'm wet thinking about it," said Susan.

"You sound like you're actually happy for her," Trish said.

"No, not happy. Let's just say I understand. Look Trish, she's like you and me."

"What do you mean?"

"I'm sure she tries new perfumes, buys lacey nightgowns, creams herself silly so she smells good and keeps her skin soft. And none of it matters. For all of our efforts to look younger and be sexy and beautiful for our husbands, we're lucky if they give us the time of day."

"But is that enough reason to be unfaithful?" Trish choked on the last word.

"Wait a minute. No one said the lady's been unfaithful.

All we know is she's having lunch with a man. Big deal! We haven't seen anything." She paused. "Besides, what if she is?"

"Susan! I can't believe you!"

"Believe it, Trish. Maybe I see things a little differently now that I've been married most of my adult life."

The waitress placed their platters on the orange place mats covered with puzzles and games to keep younger patrons busy. A quarter clinked and the shiny silver jukebox on a nearby table came to life. Strains of "Unchained Melody" drifted to them.

"Trish," the friends stared at each other, "haven't you ever been attracted to another man?"

"I love Brad. I would never be interested in another man."

"I don't doubt you love him. But that's not the question. Have you ever been attracted to another man?"

"No. I can't say I have. But . . ." the corner of Trish's mouth slithered upward.

Susan leaned closer.

"Patricia Hunter, what have you been hiding from me?"

"Well, I've never told this to anyone and I am not sure it happened, but . . ."

"But what?"

"Take it easy. I'm getting to it. I feel funny talking like this," Trish said.

Susan bolted upright. "Trish, you have my undivided attention." She looked dartingly about the diner. Then, satisfied there was no one she knew, she crossed her heart. "I swear I'll never tell a soul."

"Well, before Phillip was born, we were at a pool party. It was one of those brutally hot days when just thinking made you sweat. I'd been drinking too much sangria and as soon as my glass was empty, it was filled. This went on for hours.

After a while, joints were passed around. It was that Mexican gold stuff. Bathing suit tops started coming off and some couples threw their car keys into one pile."

"Did you?"

"*Moi?* Miss Modesty? Are you out of your mind? Anyway, between the heat, the wine and the grass, I became dizzy. Somehow, I ended up on a bed. I thought I was alone when suddenly I felt hands all over me. Not rough, but gentle. They probed everywhere."

"Then what?"

"Then I whispered, 'Brad? Is that you?' Whoever it was answered 'yes' . . . but I wasn't certain it was him. By then, it didn't matter. I was so turned on I closed my eyes and let it happen."

"And?"

Trish grinned. "It was the best lovemaking I ever experienced before . . . or since. That's why I know it wasn't Brad. It had to be someone else."

"See what I mean. You had great sex with a stranger and lived to tell about it. What harm did it do?"

"But that's not the same thing as having an affair. I mean, I didn't seek it out and besides, I'm not sure it happened."

"It happened in your mind, Trish, and that makes it real. You've kept this memory alive for eighteen years. I don't know about you, but I need something to dream about. Call it girlish fantasies. But the older I get, the more I need them."

Murmuring conversations and tinkling glasses filled the air.

"Wait a minute!" said Susan. "This happened before Phillip was born?"

"So what?"

"So how do you know Phillip is Brad's son?"

"Of course Brad's the father. You don't think . . . ?"

"Are you sure?"

It took both hands for Trish to bring the water glass to her mouth.

No two days at the lab were the same. Often, the technicians and researchers invited Phillip to help them. Dr. Sims, who ran the lab next door, was lecturing Phillip about the action of anti-inflammatory drugs on bradykinin when a scholarly man in a chocolate-brown suit appeared at the door. He held a piece of paper in his hand, looking lost.

"May I help you?" Dr. Sims asked.

The man looked at the paper again. With a Spanish accent, he asked, "Is this the laboratory of Dr. Bellman?" He distinctly separated the five syllables in *laboratory*.

"Yes, it is. I'm Dr. Sims. What can I do for you?"

The man straightened his stance, clicked his heels and became two inches taller. His thin upper lip was shadowed by an equally thin moustache that sprouted from the depression under his nose. It was not a coincidence that the lines on his tie were parallel to his moustache. A meager clump of straggly dyed black hair was pulled over the top of his head for the illusion of fullness.

"Permit me to introduce myself." He bowed. Rolling his right hand with his palm up, as well as his "RRRR's," a business card magically materialized between two fingers.

"I am Dr. Raoul Lopez-Garces. I am here to calibrate your electron microscope."

With an economy of motion and a minimum of dialogue, the former doctor/poet/political activist from Chile calibrated the lab's newest acquisition with surgical precision. Phillip watched in awe as Dr. Lopez-Garces's fingers flailed like a piano virtuoso. The task completed, the expatriate invited Phillip to talk about an enchanted world of beauty and elegance that had ended for many in torture and destruction.

Another day, another experience . . . one more chapter in the unwritten book of Phillip Hunter had come to pass. But the vicissitudes of those first few days at Parker could not compare to what lay in store for him.

It was the day before the "Fourth" and the lab was running at full tilt. Late in the morning, Frank went to Mr. Soo and Phillip.

"Boys, I've got to run a little experiment. I need fresh serum. Mr. Soo?" he nodded to the diminutive technician with the reluctant smile. "Let's show Phillip the routine. Your arm for science, if you please." Phillip watched as the black-haired man with the moon face removed his lab coat and extended his forearm. When Frank finished filling the vial with blood, they switched places and without speaking, the technician drew blood from his boss. Frank was fair.

Phillip started to walk away but Frank called to him.

"Phillip? Interested in making a donation?"

"Shit." He had hoped to escape. "I don't think I really want to, Frank. I draw the line at blood-sucking requests," he said with a frozen smile.

Frank belched a determined chuckle.

"Don't you want to contribute?"

"This is beyond the call of duty. Where's the shop steward? Uh, how often do we give at this office?"

"Every other week. Right, Mr. Soo?" he said, batting an eyelid. Before his nephew could protest, Frank took his arm and drew a sample of blood.

Leaving Mr. Soo and Phillip with arms bent, Frank walked to his office. When the door was shut, he discarded two of the glass tubes, labeling the only tube that mattered: the one with Phillip Hunter's blood. Five minutes later, a messenger arrived to pick up the red-stoppered vial. By noon, they were delivered to the Essex County Blood Bank, headed by Dr. Pat Novick, noted hematologist and geneticist.

That night, Trish had special plans for Brad. Maybe it was the result of seeing Vivian Gersten in the diner or maybe it was her conversation with Susan. Or maybe it was the memory of a pool party a long time ago. While Brad read in the den, Trish tried on an assortment of nightgowns before settling on a pink teddy.

Pleased with her choice, she got under the covers, waiting to surprise him. She touched her thigh and felt the warmth radiating from her skin. Her fingers edged closer to the metal snaps. A sudden moan escaped her lips when she felt the thick, slippery moisture flowing freely, wetting her nightgown.

Finally, Brad entered the bedroom. "Don't put the lights on, honey. I'm waiting for you," she said in a husky voice. "Sure thing," Brad answered unsuspectingly. She watched him trudge back and forth from his closet to the bathroom to the clothes hamper. He took a leak, brushed his teeth, gargled, flossed and took another leak. Finally, he turned off the light.

Brad got into his side of the bed and Trish rolled toward him. They kissed lightly and when his hands rested— and stayed—on her bare shoulders, Trish guided them to her waist.

"What's this?" he asked, feeling the sleek silk.

"What's what?" She had led him to the Promised Land and now it was his job to recognize he was there.

"What's the occasion?"

"Do we need one? Whatever happened to making

love spontaneously? Besides," she added, "it's been quite a while."

"Very funny, Trish. How long's it been? A week? Ten days?"

She pushed him away. "You're serious, aren't you! You don't even know! Well, for your information, it's been three-and-a-half weeks!" But rather than wait for his response, Trish pushed her body into his, stroking him until he got hard. "Don't rush it. I want to enjoy this."

"Don't you always?" he asked.

She grimaced.

"Brad," she pulled the teddy over her hips, "what's happened to the heat? The passion?"

"I'll show you passion, baby." Brad supported himself over her near-naked body, pumping in and out. Sweat formed in the small of his back, beading along his forehead. Just as she caught his rhythm, he gasped and cried out, his passion depleted.

The lightness of Brad's body became heavy as he lay on top of her, panting. She blinked, remembering how it was when making love meant something else.

3

❦❦

A high pressure system from Canada brought welcome relief to the sweltering days of the previous week. The terraced backyard, shaded by black walnut and tulip poplars, offered vantage points to watch the many guests at Susan and Rick Sturnweiss's annual July Fourth bash. Brad found the bar at the far end of the pool, and, with drink in hand, surveyed the early arrivals. Trish made Brad promise to mingle, but he preferred hearing Lance Beckworth tell Kip Hastings how good his business was or listening to Judge Wilbur DuPaul joke with Connie Turpen.

"She's something, Brad," Trish's boss, Steve Sadler, said.

"Huh? How's the new office?"

"You should've seen the way she handled the G.C. Trish caught him in plenty of mistakes. Christ, she ran circles around the architect, to boot. If it weren't for her, I'd be in the old dump."

"She's good at organizing."

Steve scratched his nose and sucked air through his teeth.

"Did she tell you the way she got Siemans to pull a CAT scan on route to some hospital in Nebraska and send it to us because she got the office ready early? That takes smarts and lots of moxie. I hope no one steals her away."

"Yeah, she's great." Brad sipped his drink.

"I hope you know how great she really is. I do."

Inside the sprawling ranch-style house, Vivian Gersten caught Trish coming out of the master bathroom. It had an imported marble floor, gold spigots, and mirrored walls and ceiling.

"I've got to tell someone."

"Tell someone what, Viv?"

"I did it!"

"Did what?"

"I did it with Chris. You know . . ." her eyes widened prompting Trish to fill in the missing name.

"The guy you were with in the diner?"

"You saw us?"

"Uh, you weren't exactly invisible."

"Damn. I'm so oblivious. He's Megan's ophthalmologist."

"I know."

"Is that all you can say? I thought you'd be happy for me. It's been so long since I've made love; I didn't know if I still worked."

"Well . . . do you?"

Vivian whispered in her ear. "I come thinking about him. When we do it, I have to put a pillow over my head."

"I guess I'm glad for you, Viv, but it's . . . it's something I'd never do."

"Never say 'never', Trish. You'd be surprised at the things people do."

Phillip, Gillian, and a bunch of their friends spent the holiday at Action Park, a theme park in Great Gorge, New Jersey. During the morning, they wore crash helmets and raced around hairpin loops in dragsters, drove Miami Vice speedboats, and negotiated steep dirt hills and gullies on motorcross bikes. Afterward, they glided down pretzel-shaped water flumes on mats and rubber tubes, and floated through large pipes propelled by rushing water, ending in a ten-foot drop into an icy pool. Whenever they could, Phillip and Gillian sneaked a kiss.

Twilight approached and the day's warmth escaped with the fleeing sun. Gillian and Phillip changed into dry clothes, telling their friends they would meet at the band shell in an hour. They walked arm in arm, oblivious to the clamor of jeers, oohs, and ahs that followed them.

The path led up a steep hill to an isolated area where they sat on a large boulder and watched the final amber rays disappear in the distant horizon. Isolated clouds hung overhead, tinged with purple and splashes of fiery sienna. The warm colors of waning daylight forecast another beautiful day.

"Did you know the sun set a minute ago?" he asked.

"What are you talking about?" Her arm was outstretched. "The sun's right there."

"Not true! We're witnessing something called 'parallax.' The sun's already set, we're seeing its reflection due to the curvature of the earth. It's like seeing it through a mirror."

As he spoke, the sun vanished.

"Oh yeah," she said. "And I suppose the moon, over there, is an illusion, too?"

"Of course not. That's real. And speaking of illusions and things that appear real but aren't. . . ."

"Yes?"

She moistened her lips and closed her eyes.

"Do I look like my dad?"

She sat up.

"Of course you do," she said studying his face.

"Think about it. Ron and Todd have straight hair. Mine's the same color as Todd's but the texture's completely different. And another thing . . ." he said holding his hands out in

32

the silver moonlight, "my skin, it's . . . it's different than theirs."

"How?"

"Darker." He nodded, as if ending a debate he had been having with himself for some time. "Yup, it's definitely darker. And my teeth are . . ."

"Are what? What are you talking about?"

"Everyone in my family has perfect teeth except me. I was the only one who needed braces."

"Phillip, what brought this on? You're scaring me. You make it sound like you're adopted or something."

"I have a bad feeling. Sometimes I turn around real quick, to see if someone's following me, but no one's there."

Phillip stood up and took a few steps.

He turned and flapped his arms.

"Gilly, haven't you ever gotten some crazy notion in your head that you couldn't get rid of? The kind that plays over and over like a broken record." His chest sunk. "It gets to you after a while."

She extended her arms to him.

They kissed long and hard, their tongues exploring each other's mouth. Phillip pressed his body against hers, his clasped fingers pulling her in tight. Like leaded lures, his eyes were clamped shut.

"Gilly?"

"Yes?"

"Don't let go."

4

❦❦

"**A**re you sure?" Frank asked.

"You know how these analyzers work. There's no mistake."

Without another comment, Frank replaced the receiver. He felt a sudden chill and blew into his hands for warmth. Then he pulled open the bottom drawer of his desk and fished beneath reams of old reports. Touching the familiar shape, he retrieved the bottle of Jack Daniels he had put there for emergencies.

He filled the bottom of a 500 milliliter glass beaker parked on his desk, emptying it in one dusty swallow. The amber liquor burned his throat. He felt a searing glow engulf the sides of his stomach. He poured another.

Halfway through his second laboratory goblet of bourbon, his eyes rested on a book cover. An emaciated man barely filling the seat of a wheelchair looked at him. His black hair covered his forehead and he wore glasses with a simple frame. He was dressed in a dark sports jacket, blue oxford shirt and a red-striped tie, all of which looked too big for him. Once upon a time, long ago, they might have fit. Bony arms with crippled fingers lay like wooden blocks on his lap. A blue-black sky filled with an array of stars, a mere speck of the galaxy, served as his backdrop.

Frank thumbed through the book; it was on astrophysics, on the nature of time and the universe. The jacket cover said that its author, Stephen W. Hawking, who suffered from Lou Gehrig's disease, was one of the great minds of the twentieth century. A sentence grabbed his attention: "Today we still yearn to know why we are here and where we came from." The book was called *A Brief History of Time*.

"You can't barge into our house with a fantastic story like that. Have you lost your mind?" Trish asked.

"I said, 'Maybe he's not your son.' I'm not even sure. But once I found out I had to tell you." Frank coughed, wishing he were anyplace else but there. A fetid odor came from his underarms.

"Trish, calm down." Brad squeezed her forearm. "Let Frank explain this thing about the hairs one more time. I'm not following him."

"Well, I am, and the whole thing's preposterous. Just because his son . . . ."

"Trish, let . . . him . . . speak."

So, one more time, Frank explained how Phillip became interested in the genetically bred mice used at Parker for most of the experiments.

"You mean you order them from a catalogue?" Brad interrupted.

"Fed Ex'ed the next day."

Frank continued.

He explained how he plucked a hair from Phillip's head and placed it under the microscope.

"So when he saw the two tiny bumps, these protein moieties, I explained he had AB blood. It was supposed to be harmless. Who knew *this* could come of it?"

"And the bit about our hairs? Where does that fit in?"

Trish stood with her arms folded across her chest, her fists clenched.

"I'm not surprised he did it, given Phillip's curiosity."

"What'd he do, Frank?" Brad's temples pulsed.

"Phillip took a hair from Trish's brush and one wedged between your comb, Brad. When you think about it, it was the natural thing to do. He wanted to match your blood types with his. But when I looked through the microscope, I knew immediately there was a problem. That's the day I came here in the rain."

"At the time, I thought you had lost it, coming in the pouring rain to check the sauna's connectors. But it made sense knowing how Myrna gets. That's when you went to our bathroom and took pieces of our hair."

"I had to be sure. Phillip's samples showed you had Type B and Trish had O. But it's only a screening technique."

"What's a screening technique, Frank?" Brad asked.

"It's a test reliable most of the time but not all the time. In this particular case, blood type determined from hair samples is only ninety-five percent accurate."

"Can it be used as evidence?" Trish asked.

"Not at all. Five percent error's too excessive. It might be used to eliminate a suspect rather than convict one. More accurate tests exist for identifying criminals."

"Jesus. You're scaring the daylights out of us. I'm sure Phillip's ours," Brad said.

"He probably is. I'm only telling you what I saw. Someone could've used your brush, Trish, or your comb," he said looking at Brad. "It's probably a fluke."

"If it's a fluke, why'd you bother telling us?" Brad asked. "No parent wants to hear this; it's so far-fetched."

"Is that all you have to say?" Trish turned to her brother-in-law. "Look, Frank, I don't know what your game is, what you think you're trying to do here, but it won't work. The implication's preposterous. Don't you think I know who my son is? I certainly don't need you or anyone else to question what I know to be true in my heart and soul. A mother knows who her child is, it's that simple."

"Trish, I'm sure it's wrong, but how can you ignore what Frank's saying?"

"Have you lost it? Phillip's our son. You were at the delivery. You saw him come out of me. This makes no sense." Trish's eyes bugged out of their sockets, her neck veins stretched in tight cords. She slapped the couch.

Frank stood up. "I think I should leave, now."

"Great, Frank, you waltz into our home, tell us Phillip may not be ours and leave when we're discussing it. Why'd you do it? Have you lost your sense?"

"Trish, I did what I thought was right. I'm not saying Phillip isn't your son, there's a chance he isn't. Take a blood test and you'll know for sure."

Trish met Frank eye-to-eye. "Prove Phillip is ours? You've been hovering over beakers too long. The fumes have liquefied your common sense. A bona fide man would've known what to do." Frank's eyes dropped. The air sizzled.

Brad's tongue crept over his lower lip, circled it and disappeared.

"Trish. Since Frank's sprung this on us, maybe we should take the test to simply clear it up."

She sprang toward him.

"What? You, too? The matter's closed. Good-bye, Frank."

The two men watched her hike up the stairs. Each one started to speak, then halted. Frank moved backward toward the foyer.

Brad scratched his head. "Frank, I can't . . . if what you're saying is . . . I've got to digest this."

37

"I thought you should know, that's all. It could be a mistake." Frank's airborne words, pods of doubt, drifted and floated and then evaporated.

Brad heard the front door shut. He looked about the room aimlessly. Then his eyes rested on the bookshelves. "Why you sneaky son-of-a-bitch," he said, springing from the couch. Brad snatched the photo album and flipped the pages, stopping at a picture he had glanced at countless times before. He saw it differently, now.

It was summertime; they were sitting around a pool. Todd was one. He had near-platinum hair neatly combed, and was seated on Trish's lap. Ron was balanced on his knee while Phillip, with his dark, wavy hair, stood between them. Brad studied their faces. Though their coloring was different, Ron and Todd had similar features, much like his when he was young. But Phillip? How could he ever think Phillip looked like any of them? His lips were fuller, his nose larger, and there was something about his eyes. They were set unmistakably deeper than his brothers'. The longer he studied the picture, the more confused he became.

Lifelines crisscrossed, memories became jumbled. Brad yanked his hair then wiped his palms on the couch. He strode to the hall mirror and stared.

Convinced of his next step, he mounted the gallows.

"Trish, we have to deal with this." He found her crying on their bed.

"There's nothing to deal with," she said between tears. "Phillip's our son. Do you doubt that for a minute?"

"No, not really."

"Then what's to discuss? Besides, Frank's jealous. You know how disappointed he is in Kevin. He's made it perfectly clear. Doesn't even try to hide it. The boy's a loser and since Frank's been working with Phillip, it's become more apparent to him."

"Hey, you think Frank's doing this maliciously?"

"Could be. Remember, Frank was thrown out of the University of Chicago for falsifying data. How do we know he hasn't screwed something up? He's done it before. For that matter, maybe he's lying? The guy can't be trusted."

"But, Trish, you know he was under a lot of pressure raising Kevin. He said he didn't do anything wrong; it was someone else's research."

"Oh, yeah! Then why'd they throw him out? You're the one who's always saying leopards don't change their spots."

Sleep eluded Brad. The alarm clock's green luminescent dial kept him up all night. Bleary eyed, he stared at Trish. How was she able to sleep? By 5:15 A.M., he had to do something.

The early morning sky took on the pale hues of sunrise with distant beiges melding into the lingering darknesses. Avoiding Phillip's Jeep on the side of the driveway, Brad pulled his car out of the garage. He needed to think. There was a solution to this, there had to be one. He had to find it before it drove him crazy. Brad headed north, the opposite direction of his business.

He opened the window and the cool crisp morning air filled the car. By nightfall, the weight of Frank's story would make breathing more difficult.

He pulled into a wooded area and parked. The smell of flowers and dew wafted the air. Crickets chirped and birds called to each other, spreading messages in secret languages. Brad trudged forward then stopped, anticipating some divine intervention, some "sign" telling him what to do. A burning bush. Anything. But none came.

An orange sunrise gave way to a sky of pastel blue, inlaid with ruby wisps and floating necklaces of clouds. In time, a stream of cars hurtled down the road behind him, ignoring the lonely figure standing in the woods.

If it would have helped, Brad would have driven further. He would have done anything to have cancelled Phillip's genetic lesson. By telling them, Frank expunged his responsibility, his guilt. But at what price? Their lives might now be altered forever. And for what? A mistake? Or was it jealousy, as Trish suggested?

5

❦❦

The next night, Phillip phoned Gillian.

"I've got to see you."

"Anything wrong?"

"I'll tell you when I see you."

Minutes later, Phillip picked her up, and they drove to the oval park dedicated to war heroes in front of Livingston High School.

"What's wrong?" she asked as they plopped onto a wooden bench. Fireflies flashed their luminescent tails throughout the park to the distant shouting and laughter, while a small band of boys played with a fluorescent frisbee in the fading light.

"I don't know. It's Frank. He's been acting weird. Since he came in this morning, he hasn't stopped whistling and singing. Every time I move, he's standing next to me, like he's my shadow or something. One time, I turned to put a bottle away and bumped right into him. I nearly dropped a gallon of acid on him."

"That doesn't sound so strange. He's looking after you."

"C'mon, Gilly. But that's not all. I can't put my finger on it."

"Is there something else?"

"My folks. Dinner tonight was so bizarre."

"Yeah? What'd your mom serve?" He jabbed her lightly on the shoulder.

"I'm bummed out and you're making jokes."

"Sorry." She touched his hand.

"Anyway, it's not so much what they said, but how they looked at me. They stared at me like . . . like I was a stranger."

"You know what I think? I think your imagination's getting the best of you."

"Something's up and I don't know what it is."

"I do," she said, grabbing between his legs.

Gillian and Phillip grappled, ignoring the window-rattling gas guzzlers that pin-wheeled around Memorial Drive, while, at the same time, Brad agonized in his bed. He focused on the air conditioner's clicking compressor; he never realized how loud it was. A branch from the white birch rubbed the aluminum siding in tempo to the metronomic rasps of doomed cicadas. Moonshadows danced on the slanted ceiling, reminding Brad of the broomsticks in *Fantasia*. And all the while, Trish slept.

. . . *extended stays in L.A. Twenty years ago. Flight attendant on the West Coast run. Handsome pilots and hotels. Pot parties. Pacific sunsets. Barefoot walks on the white sand. Millions of stars. Was she . . . alone?*

He awoke with a jolt in a lost haze, unsure of where he was. The sheet was drenched with sweat. Whose son did he raise? Sleep still eluded him.

"Trish?" he said shaking her lightly, "I need to talk with you. Wake up."

"I'm sleeping. Can't it wait?"

"No, it can't. We've got to do it."

"Do what?"

"Take blood tests."

42

With surprising cat-like quickness, she whipped her pillow from under her head and swung at his face. He dodged the hit.

"We need to take the blood tests." The words pummelled her senses.

"Are you out of your mind?"

"Stop shrieking, you'll wake the children."

"Good. They should hear what their father's trying to do."

"Do? What am I trying to do? Discover if our son's really ours? How can you dismiss what Frank said?"

"Easily. He's an asshole. He wants to hurt us. What gets me is how'd he think we'd respond to this cock-and-bull story? Anyone with half a brain knows it's ridiculous."

Yet why had flashbacks of the same pool party she had discussed with Susan resurfaced ever since Frank's visit? Splashes of faces and drops of sentences fused into fears she once managed to bury.

"But that's why I think he's on the level. Frank Bellman is a first-rate scientist, someone who's trained to discover the truth."

"Ha!"

Brad ignored her. "If he didn't think it were possible, he'd never have come here. Look, this is getting us nowhere. Let's take the blood test. It'll probably show that this is a big mistake and we can forget it ever happened."

"Brad. I've forgotten about it already. Phillip is ours." She rubbed her eyes.

"I just want to check it out."

"Do you love me?"

"Of course I love you."

"Then how can you pursue this?"

"What does love have to do with it? I'm trying to find out who my son is, that doesn't mean I don't love you."

"To me, it's a question of love and respect. I've never

asked you for anything before. What good would a blood test do? Please just drop it."

The early morning sun sent probing shafts of light through the vertical blinds and one golden ray caressed Trish's face. For an instant, time was suspended. Maybe it was the tilt of her head or the way she crinkled her brow when she was upset, but after twenty years, she looked the same to him. She was a flight attendant on a Northwest Airlines flight from Minneapolis. He had noticed her the moment he dropped into his seat. His eyes followed her as she walked up and down the aisle, assisting passengers with their coats and bags. Maybe this time, he would fly without turning green.

Buffeting drafts tossed the plane. Strapped to the chair, he clutched the armrests. She handed him what might have been his last meal. The steaming goulash, apple-green peas and water-sogged potatoes, all drenched in a brown gel, did him in.

"Here, let me help you," she said.

"Thanks, I'm . . ." then he buried his head in the half-filled bag.

"Drink this. The ginger ale will settle your stomach."

When the other passengers were served, she returned.

"Are you feeling better?"

Brad managed a sickly nod.

"What's your name?" he asked when he felt better.

"Trish. Trish Treat."

"Sounds like what kids say on Halloween," he said.

The light shifted from her face. Three children and two decades later, it was no longer a bucking plane, it was his life.

"Trish, this is not a bad dream that's going away when you wake up. It's a fucking nightmare."

"Why are you falling apart over a stupid piece of hair?"

"That stupid piece of hair may mean I'm not his father. Maybe you can live with the fact that you might not be his mother, but I can't."

Like a summer squall that suddenly appeared and left just as quickly, her dark cloud lifted. She leaned toward him and with the barest touch of her fingertips on his stubbled skin, drew his face to hers. Their lips touched.

"I get it now. You're going through one of those cave man macho things where you need to know where your precious sperm ended up. You'll get over it."

Before he could say anything, she pulled the covers over her head and was asleep in seconds.

Phillip spent the next day working with Mr. Soo. They extracted serum from lab mice injected with cancerous tumors; it was part of an experiment designed to prevent tumors from metastasizing.

Bleary-eyed at day's end, he found his uncle. "I'm finished, Frank. Everyone's left. Do you want me to wait?"

"No thanks. I'm meeting some hotshots from the F.D.A. They're coming from Washington to discuss ways to test orphan drugs more cheaply." Phillip frowned. "There's a need to develop drugs for handfuls of people with rare diseases. Parker avoids that kind of work because we lose money on them."

"Is that the only reason drug companies make pills?"

"Most of the time, Phillip. We answer to our stockholders like any other company."

"I thought research is for helping people."

"People and pocketbooks. That's the real world, Phillip."

"Maybe they'll have a solution so you can help more people. Anyway, have a good meeting." Frank listened to

Phillip's footsteps in the empty hall. Calculating the time it took for the elevator, Frank walked to the window and saw him drive off.

Satisfied he wasn't coming back, Frank went to Soo's lab bench and removed two glass tubes plus two disposable syringes. He placed them on a tray adding alcohol wipes, Band-Aids and an eighteen-inch piece of yellow latex tubing, which he found on the counter. Frank returned to his office and waited for his visitors. Moments later, there was a knock on the lab door.

"Who's first?"

Brad and Trish drove away in a cocoon of silence. After some minutes, she turned to him.

"I can't believe you made me do this." Brad's eyes never left the road. Sparks flew from her electrified stare. He jiggled with his seat belt.

"Why?" She clutched her arms and hunched her shoulders, huddling into a frail ball.

"I had to," he answered.

They moved about the house, trying to keep busy. Brad read but found himself staring at the same page for half an hour. Trish glared at the television, oblivious to what played.

Unable to follow the program, she sought refuse in a hot shower. She stared at her size-ten feet while the pulsating water pelted her back. When the wash cloth pressed the sore spot on her arm she winced, reminded of her blood filling the tube.

Trish wrapped her body in a large towel, toga-fashion, and grabbed a smaller one, wrapping her hair in a turban. She brushed her teeth. Deep in thought, she didn't hear Brad tiptoe behind her. Lips lightly touched the nape of her neck and the hairs on her arm stood up. Goose bumps rose over her body.

"You're still wet," he said and pulled the towel off. Brad dabbed the glistening drops and then let go of the towel. Bare except for her headdress, she watched in the mirror as Brad journeyed down her back, licking her skin. Her nipples turned to hardened erasers. She wet her middle finger and massaged them in slow, circular motions as Brad bent below her view. She closed her eyes.

Brad bit her thigh and she moaned. With a firm grip, he rotated her body to face him. They exchanged glances but as he lowered his head, she pried loose.

"What gives?" Brad leaned back, still on his knees.

"You think that'll make it better? Make me forgive you?" She stood tall, hands planted on her hips, her breasts joggling as she spoke.

Brad flashed a twisted smirk.

"I thought it would break the tension, make you feel better."

"Thanks. When was the last time you cared how I felt? And where do you get off trying to ruin our family? I married you because you were kind and considerate. You were different than the others. I should've known all men are the same."

Brad cocked forward, poised to stand, then collapsed on his haunches.

"Where do you come off talking about ruining the family? Everything I do is for the family. I work hard to give you and the children what you need. I don't do anything for myself. So I resent. . . ."

She grabbed her ears.

"That's bullshit. You're so full of you yourself you can't see that you're still trying to get your father's approval . . . and he was dead before I met you. You think burying yourself in your goddamned business and spending every free minute with the boys makes everything all right? Well, I count, too. You've ignored my feelings for years. You care more about strangers than me. I wanted more but I figured you couldn't give it to me, so I accepted it—until now. Tearing our family apart because a flunky, third-rate scientist thinks Phillip's not ours is where I draw the line."

Brad slumped to the floor, his head dropped into his hands. The floor swayed and he tasted bile. His eyes crawled from behind his fingers. Like a snail, he rose.

"You have to understand that everything I do is for the good of the family. I scratch and claw my way through every day so you and our children, and I mean *our* children, have the best lives I can give you."

"But I work. . . ."

"I'm not finished. This is not about my father or what I did to please or displease him. That's in the past. No, Trish, this is only about one thing: We might have a son out there and I want to know he's all right, that he's taken care of."

In the morning Frank analyzed reams of reports, but after the phone call, he could no longer concentrate. He looked about the lab. Phillip was helping Soo cut mice sections snap-frozen in liquid nitrogen and stored at $-75°$ C, with a cryostat. They were about to perform a direct immuno-fluorescence analysis and would be busy for hours. Even if he wanted to help, he couldn't. Not now. He had to leave.

When Frank got there, the narrow driveway was blocked by a UPS truck, forcing him to wait in his car, trapped with his thoughts. Three minutes seemed to take forever.

Frank's chubby legs weighed him down as he plodded into the showroom. Katie greeted him with an infectious smile, coercing one back.

"Hi! I don't know if you remember me but we met at. . . ."

"Why you're Dr. Bellman. Of course I remember. It was at last year's Christmas party."

"You have a good memory, er. . . ."

"Katie."

"Yes, Katie. Anyway, is Mr. Hunter here?"

"Yes, he is, Dr. Bellman. I'll page him for you."

Hearing over the intercom that it was his brother-in-law, Brad vaulted down the stairs. His heart hammered. With no greeting, Brad ushered Frank into his office. Even before the door shut, he held both hands up in supplication.

"Well?"

Frank's frown told him the test results. "I'm sorry, Brad. I don't know what to say. I feel responsible for this mess. What can I do to help?"

"Help? Tell me there's some mistake. Tell me this never happened, or that it's a terrible joke."

"Boy, do I wish I could, but it's not. Not only were the DNA tests repeated, which are infallible, but they ran a series of protein tests also showing no match. It's irrefutable. Phillip is not your son."

"Then who's his father? Was it when Trish was still flying to L.A.?"

"Wait a second! Is *that* what you think? That Trish was fooling around?"

"How else can you explain it?"

"But I thought you understood why I came to you in the first place. If it was simply a case of your not being the father, I never would have said a word. Believe me, that's none of my business."

"What the hell are you talking about? I don't get it."

"Brad, Trish isn't Phillip's mother. Neither of you are the parents. Phillip belongs to someone else."

Brad sat down. The normally inaudible tick of the

clock clicked away the seconds. He didn't blink, and he barely breathed. Like time-lapse photography, Brad Hunter could only frame one abstraction at a time, until the truth came to him.

"Then whose is he? How could this have happened? Where's *my* son?"

"The only explanation that makes any sense is that your son was somehow switched by chance at the hospital. You and Trish brought the wrong baby home."

"What can we do?"

"Why do anything? Nothing's changed."

"Maybe you're right. Why should this change anything? After all, Trish and I raised Phillip—as though he was our real son. I mean, doesn't that make him our son?"

"I think so. Listen Brad, you're the only one who knows the results of the tests."

"So?"

"So, no one else has to know. I had to tell you, but let it stop here. Tell Trish everything checked out fine. And Phillip doesn't suspect a thing."

"I don't know, Frank."

"There's nothing to think about. Forget the whole thing."

"What the fuck's wrong with you? You march in here, telling me Phillip is not mine out of some misplaced duty to the truth, and then in the next breath, you tell me to forget about it?"

"I'm just trying to be helpful."

Brad stood. "You've been help enough, Frank. I need to think about this."

Frank watched Brad struggle to the window and gape at the passing cars. He waited for him to say something else, to curse, to scream. Frank opened and closed his fists; he braced himself for whatever would come next, but Brad stared in silence. Easing backward one step at a time, Frank's hand found the brass-plated door knob and in a flash, he was gone. He spent the rest of the afternoon in a bar with fly-specked pictures of long-ago sports figures on the wall, drinking gin and tonics, which he soon lost track of.

Brad couldn't recall how long he had leaned against the window.

"Trish, stay there. Frank was here, and we need to talk."

"It's bad, isn't it?" she asked, but the phone had gone dead. For a moment, she tried to tackle the mound of insurance forms on her desk, but then found herself waiting, as if in a trance.

When she saw Brad's Volvo, she bolted to the parking lot. Inside the car, Brad repeated every detail of his meeting with Frank, while Trish listened without saying a single word. When he grew silent, she continued to gaze out the windshield. Her lips paled.

She whipped around. "Brad Hunter! We don't have to do anything. Phillip will never hear about this! Never! Do you understand me?"

Brad slammed the steering wheel. Trish jumped. His thoughts were chaotic.

"Trish, that was my reaction, too. I even thought of not telling *you.*"

"I wish you *hadn't.*"

"Since when do you want me to keep anything from you?" She shook her head.

"I considered keeping this to myself, but then I realized we have a son out there. I need to know who he is. It won't change how we feel toward Phillip. We raised him; we've always loved him and always will. But what's important. . . ."

Her hand darted up like a traffic cop. Her eyes widened.

"There's only one important thing and that's for you to forget this whole crazy thing. Phillip's our son, at least we agree on that. I've worked too hard to keep this family together, and you're not going to spoil it for any reason."

"But we need to find the truth."

"The truth? I just told you the truth!"

She opened the car door, and Brad watched his wife stalk away. Trish had the ability to bury her head under the covers and sleep away problems. But Brad couldn't turn his back on Phillip or on the son they never knew.

Somewhere, there was a son Brad needed to see—another son.

6

❧❧

Brad heard the jangling keys before the front door swung open. He heard the muffled steps on the carpeted stairs and his first impulse was to call his name. But he didn't. "Hey, Dad, couldn't get Mom to watch those porno flicks with you?"

"Very funny, Phil. I couldn't sleep."

Phillip scanned the screen.

"Why tapes when we were kids?"

"Dunno. I had this urge to see you, Ron, and Todd when you were little."

Phillip stepped to leave.

"Phillip? Sit down for a minute."

"What's Mom doing?"

"Sleeping."

Brad practiced this a million times. He even rehearsed in front of the mirror.

"Phillip," he said, "your mother and I spoke to Frank this week and he told us. . . ."

"Wait a sec. Is this about the hair samples?"

"You know about them?"

"Of course I do. I was the one who started the whole thing. I asked Frank about genetic breeding and before you know it, the guy was trying to make me bald."

"Then you know the hairs didn't match."

"Of course I do. It didn't make any sense to me, so I asked Frank for some help. That's when I found out."

"Found out what?" Brad asked.

"About random error. The samples I used from your bathroom showed you weren't my parents. Can you imagine that?" He shrugged his shoulders and threw his hands up in the air.

"But they didn't lie," Brad said.

"Dad, stop joking. I fit into that 5 percent error group. Don't be ridiculous, of course I'm your son. I mean. . . ."

Phillip watched for Brad's broad grin telling him what he expected to hear, what he wanted to hear. His mouth parched as his father turned his right hand over and over in his left, like he was spatulating cement. Phillip opened his lips in anticipation of what Brad was going to say, but Brad uttered no more while furiously moving his hands.

Phillip felt trapped and moved away. He rubbed the back of his head, then confronted Brad.

"Why are you staring like that, Dad? I *am* your son, aren't I? People can't tell us apart on the phone. We sound alike. We walk alike. I mean, everyone makes fun of the way we waddle side-to-side. Dad, look at me, damn it, this isn't funny."

Brad looked up, but he couldn't see clearly through his watery eyes.

"Do you remember when Frank drew blood from you and Mr. Soo?"

"Yeah. He took it from himself, too. What about it?"

"To make it look real. All he wanted was yours, he threw theirs away."

Phillip backed up, his heel bumped into a chair. He

groped until he felt the arm rest and eased his way down. He leaned forward and swallowed hard.

"Dad, what are you saying, that the hair samples were right? But, it couldn't be. It. . . ."

"The night Frank told you about the feds coming. . . ."

"Something about orphan drugs. Don't tell me. You were the. . . ."

"It was us. Your mother and I had our blood. . . ."

"Dad, be straight with me. Am I adopted?"

"If you were, Phillip, we'd have told you a long time ago. You're not adopted."

"Then what am I? Who am I?"

"Frank thinks you were accidently switched in the hospital and we took you home instead of . . . our son."

A shrill whistle escaped Phillip.

Brad got up and hugged Phillip, remembering how he longed to hold his own father. Every time he had tried, the old man would stiffen up, as if he couldn't wait to get away from his only son. Brad squeezed harder.

"I don't know what to say, it's so confusing. Your mother and I love you. We always will. We're your parents, you're our son. That's all I know."

"I know you and Mom love me. You're the best parents in the whole world. I don't want any others."

They separated.

"We feel the same way, Phillip. I wish Frank had never showed you that little trick with the hair. But he did and it can't be undone."

Phillip covered his mouth, then stretched the skin on his face so that it distorted his features. Frantic air escaped replaced by a calm breath. Father and son were toe-to-toe.

"Does it matter, Dad? Does it really matter?"

"Not a goddamned bit. Not for one fucking moment."

They squared off eye-to-eye. Brad draped his arm on Phillip's shoulder. "One day, I hope a child of yours will make you as proud of him as I am of you."

Phillip kissed his father. It wasn't a peck that fathers sometimes coerce their sons to give as they get older, it was heartfelt—a real kiss.

Brad glanced at his watch. "Hey, I've got to get to sleep. Don't stay up too late."

In his room, Phillip paused in front of his wooden dresser. There was a picture of a man and three boys standing in front of a log cabin on a grassy clearing, somewhere in Idaho. It was taken a few years ago when they had gone camping and white-water rafting down the Salmon River. Phillip had passed this picture a thousand times. But now, a stranger looked back at him. Who was with his brothers? What would he tell them?

He got into bed and picked up the phone. He didn't care that it was late; she answered it on the first ring.

"You won't believe it, Gilly. I was right."

"About what?" she asked dreamily.

"About everybody looking at me weird-like." He repeated the conversation he just had with his father, panting by the time he was finished.

"That's terrible. Are you okay?"

"I think so. I only found out ten minutes ago. Maybe I'll feel differently tomorrow, but for now, I'm fine."

"What're you going to do about it?"

"There's nothing to do. I love my parents, and when they're not fighting, my brothers are great. I just can't wait to see you."

"Me, too," Gillian said, "g'night."

✿✿

"**M**ay I help you?" asked Trish Hunter. She had run Dr. Sadler's office for many years and had a knack for sizing up people right away. The man before her was in his early twenties with hair slicked back and a two-day stubble. It was clear to her he was neither a patient nor a delivery man. One whiff of his ripe scent caused her to draw back.

"Yes, ma'am. May I please speak with Dr. Sadler? He called my establishment about waste disposal," the man said in a gruff Bronx accent. He wore a pale pink monogrammed satin shirt buttoned without a tie, black linen pants and shiny cowboy boots with swirls of inset rhinestones.

"I'm Mrs. Hunter, Dr. Sadler's office manager. You are . . . ?"

"Vinnie."

"Vinnie, what?"

He wrinkled his nose and cocked his head to the left, à la Stallone, "Vinnie Saducci." Saying his name, he automatically scratched his crotch on the order of baseball players before an entire ballpark. Trish held back a laugh, and imagined him practicing the "move" in front of a mirror.

"What's this about, Vinnie?"

"Medical wastes."

"I don't think the doctor's interested, Vinnie. We follow OSHA's regulations to the letter."

"But the doc's the one who called."

"I see. Wait here while I ask the doctor."

Trish pressed the coded buttons on the intercom while Vinnie reached for the latest copy of *Architectural Digest.*

"Uh huh. Okay. Uh huh." Trish replaced the almond-colored handle. "Won't you come with me, Vinnie?"

She led him to the yellow staff room decorated with blue and green graphics that ran around the walls like racing stripes. Vinnie hiked up his pant legs so as not to ruin the crease before sitting down. Trish sat opposite.

"Let's get one thing straight, I have read every piece of paper that's crossed my desk about hazardous wastes and this office is in full compliance."

"Mrs. Hunter, I'm not here to check what you're doing. I'm sure it's just like you says. But we got a call from your boss 'cause the cleaning lady found stained gauze in the trash."

"It's okay to be there, Vinnie. There's nothing wrong with that. Disposables from people with AIDS or those who test HIV positive are handled differently. We're very careful here."

"Hey, you and I both know that, but the little ladies who clean your office don't. They're scared stiff they're going to catch it and die. That's why I'm here, to guarantee their safety."

Vinnie described the stringent measures his company took, which exceeded federal requirements for the removal of contaminated wastes. Nearing the end of his practiced speech, he produced a Xeroxed schedule of his company's fees.

Trish took the paper.

"You treat the stuff like it's plutonium. Don't you think using cartons twice the size necessary, then irradiating it before burning it, is overkill? We couldn't collect this much waste in three months, let alone every other week."

"You can never be too careful, Mrs. Hunter, especially when the lives of innocent workers are at stake. Your boss should know the cleaning people have been instructed to report every infraction they see. We got a hotline to OSHA; they want to know about these kinds of situations."

"Vinnie, do you know how big the fines are?"

He beamed.

"Yeah, like signing bonuses to play in the major leagues. That's precisely what we want to save you. Remember, Mrs. Hunter, where would we be without the little people? They've got families, too. *Capice?*"

"I *capice* very well, Vinnie. This sounds like blackmail to me. I'll get back to you after I speak with Dr. Sadler."

They walked toward the door when he wheeled.

"One last thing you should know, Mrs. Hunter. We're the only carters licensed in this county, and our prices go up next week. Don't wait too long before calling. G'bye, Mrs. Hunter. *Tempus fugit.*"

Trish watched him saunter away, mortified at how vulnerable he made her feel. Upset, she swept the office clean of Vinnie's lingering odor with a squirt or two of Lysol spray.

Later that day, Trish explained the details of Vinnie's visit to Steve Sadler while he took off his white lab coat. Trim and muscular from his regular workouts at the gym, he looked more athlete than doctor. In his mid-forties like Brad, there wasn't a wrinkle on his face or a gray hair in his thick brown mane. She thought it was because of his vegetarian diet, but, it could have been good genes.

"Trish, our hands are tied. You did a terrific job setting up the office to OSHA's regulations. The cleaning lady found one stained gauze. . . ."

"But that's not in violation. It's only a problem with fluids from known. . . ."

"But she doesn't know that. The papers and television have scared people to death. Their histrionics have pushed us back to the Dark Ages—and for no reason. If they only knew how hard it was to catch the disease. The union's got us by the balls."

"Union my foot, the government has created a legal business for the Mafia," she said.

"It doesn't matter. We can't afford to take a chance. Call your Vinnie 'the Eloquent' and begin the service. *Capice?*"

"I'll do it, but I don't like it."

"I don't either, but you can't always do what you like. By the way, are you all right?"

Trish looked at him quizzically.

"Why do you ask?"

He pointed to the crook in her arm. "You've obviously had a blood test. Anything I should know about?"

Trish looked at the telltale Band-Aid. She blushed.

"Nothing serious, I hope."

"Could be. I'll let you know."

There were two hiatuses during the year when Brad could control the pace of his business, judge its needs, and enact change. Orders ceased after New Year's, and for the six weeks between July Fourth and summer's end. His was a Christmas-oriented business, and he needed large inventories for the fall. Brad inspected his plant with his shipping manager, Tommy Donovan, who had been with him since the business was housed in Newark.

Tommy was a burly, red-haired man who, on the slightest dare, would chew the bottle after he finished his beer. He grew up in the Ironbound section of Newark, which was ruled by gangs whose only education came from petty larceny and thieving among themselves. For fun, Tommy and his friends would march into a store wielding bats and snow-tire chains, and take whatever they wanted. One day, a Latino from a rival gang wanted a cut from Tommy's boys; he claimed they strayed into his territory. Tommy had other ideas and plunged a knife into his chest. The boy died and sixteen-year-old Tommy served two years in juvenile detention.

Against Trish's judgment, Brad hired Tommy. He saw a spark in his eye that reminded Brad of his own hunger to succeed. Tommy needed a chance and fortunately for him, Brad trusted his instincts. That was fifteen years ago.

"Boss, we're doing real good," Tommy said as they went into the room with the lucite Christmas tree lights.

"Yeah, I expect big things from the new catalogue—if it ever gets done."

"Aw, I knew you was a winner the first time I met you, Boss." He playfully slapped Brad on the back. "I'll clear the area on the far wall for the sockets. When d'you think they'll get here, Boss?"

"Sid called this morning and said the first shipment's coming Monday. After that, he'll send twenty thousand a week for the next three months. That should be enough for this season."

"Right-o. Next time Sid gives you a problem, Boss, just tell me and I'll straighten him out for you." Tommy jabbed the air, shadow-boxing on his toes.

"Tommy, you wouldn't hit an old man, would you?"

"Boss, I'd finish off anybody you told me to. Age don't make no difference. A rat's gotta be treated like a rat."

* * *

61

"Phillip . . . I . . . I . . ." Frank stammered.

"It's okay, Frank. It's not your fault. I don't know how it happened but it did. You're not to blame."

"You're taking this better than me."

"Frank, eventually, I would've found out. In a way, you did me a favor."

"Maybe so. But nonetheless, I feel responsible."

"You shouldn't. Besides, I'm glad it was you. A stranger wouldn't have cared as much. Thanks."

"That's rich! I discover you've got bogus parents and you thank me. You're some kid. Your parents are damned lucky." Frank reached for his mouth, wishing he could take back the remark. Who were Phillip's parents, now?

"I have a favor to ask, Frank."

"Sure, what is it?"

"I finished everything for today. Could I leave early?"

Frank checked his watch.

"It's only twelve-thirty."

"I know. I really did finish everything; the animals are fed, and Mr. Soo and I finished the last paraffin sections for microscopic inspection. And the glassware's laid out for Monday's experiments."

Frank smiled at Phillip and flicked his wrist.

"Gee, thanks, Uncle Frank. You're great."

With the afternoon free, Phillip could have visited the ice cream parlor where Gillian worked for the summer. She would have loved the surprise. He could have gone to the town pool and swum laps. Or he could have shot baskets, pounding the ball on the sticky, tar driveway until he conked out from exhaustion. But he did none of those. Phillip started for home but never got there.

An invisible force took over. Phillip missed the turn for Hobart Gap Road and drove through the twisted roads of the South Mountain Reservation. With the windows rolled down, he listened to the *Permanent Waves* tape of his favorite Canadian rock group, a band named Rush. Past Pleasant Valley Way, his Jeep strained in fourth gear chugging up the steep hill so he down-shifted into second. Cement barricades served as the median divider, protecting drivers in both directions from the deadly curves that had claimed too many.

With no goal in mind, he turned right and found himself in the parking lot of a deer sanctuary. Phillip nosed his Jeep forward until the bumper nudged the tar-painted log that served as a barrier. There were few cars there.

Between the log and the metal fence, a woman held a child in one hand and threw grain with the other. The little girl reached out, tempting a fawn to eat from her hand. Digging out a quarter, Phillip walked to what used to be a bubble gum machine and inserted the coin into the slot. He turned the knob and cupped his hand under the metal door, lifting it slowly to catch the grain before any fell onto the ground where missed handfuls were already scattered.

He strolled away from the people who were milling around. The hot summer day caused most of the deer to seek relief under the trees in back of the preserve.

Phillip stopped. He saw a doe camouflaged in the foliage a few feet away. Her fawn was beside her. The mother deer watched as Phillip drew near. She sat regally with her head held high, ready to protect her baby. Her brown eyes missed nothing. All the while, the fawn playfully rolled on its back, scratching itself, unaware of Phillip or anyone else.

"Here boy. Here boy. Look what I have for you." He threw grain halfway between himself and the young deer. The doe turned her head. She was too hot to move. The fawn, on the other hand, smelled the grain and skittishly walked to it and licked it off the ground with its thin tongue.

Phillip remained still. When it was finished, he threw

more. Though the fawn dashed a few steps away, it returned to eat the kernels on the ground. Phillip repeated the process, always cutting the distance in half until the fawn was in front of him, separated only by the fence.

"C'mon. I'm not going to hurt you," he said softly, putting grain at the end of his fingers. He pushed it through the fence and held it still. Finally, it came near enough for Phillip to feel its warm breath on his hand. Its raspy tongue tickled his fingers as it darted for the food. Repeating the motion slowly, Phillip fed the bashful fawn until no grain remained. When Phillip's legs cramped and he had to stand, the deer leaped away.

Phillip took one last look, wondering if whether given the opportunity, the deer would sprint for freedom or remain in their secure paddock. He wondered what he would choose? He stared absentmindedly when screeching tires and honking horns brought him back to reality.

"Damn!" he said out loud, kicking the front tire. Phillip jumped into his Jeep. He knew what he had to do! Rush hour was three hours away, though it didn't matter, because few people traveled *to* Newark at the end of a day.

Phillip took a ticket from the automatic server at the parking garage of Beth Israel Hospital. The yellow and black striped arm lifted to let his vehicle pass. He parked on the third level and scurried to the passenger elevator. Once on the street, Phillip jaywalked and scaled the granite stairs alongside the wheelchair ramp shared by skateboarders and Rollerbladers.

Inside, a large sign hung over a wooden table: "Information/Informacion."

"Excuse me sir, could you tell me where records are kept?"

The wrinkled brown man was missing a front tooth and his short, white hair looked like a spray-painted Brillo pad. He searched the ceiling, as if the answer was there. He scoured the cavernous lobby of the brick structure for a clue.

"Records you say? Lemme see."

He deliberated a few more seconds. What would he do if there was an emergency, Phillip wondered? Phillip moved his hand, trying to coax the answer out of him.

"More likely than not, you want to check with the records clerk," he managed to say in a soft drawl.

"And where is that?" Phillip dreaded how long the answer would take.

"That would be down in the basement. It used to be down the hall," he said, pointing. Phillip's eyes followed the rawboned finger quivering like a baton in the air. "But now it's at B . . . One . . . One . . . Four," he said. Phillip gulped as the saga continued. "Take this elevator right here, the one with them shiny buttons, and go to the basement. Follow the blue line on the floor and it'll take you where you want to go. Remember, mister, the 'B' is for blue, not basement. Everybody gets that confused."

"Thank you very much, sir," Phillip said and left while the man was still speaking. Phillip pushed the button, and heard the ancient wish him "good luck." Was it a casual remark or a veiled warning meant to keep him on guard? Was Phillip entering the bowels of a medical labyrinth cluttered with brittle, cobwebbed skeletons who became lost while lugging telephone book-sized charts, never to be seen or heard from again? Was he doomed to roam uncharted, catacombed halls forever?

Phillip followed the blue line. Most of the doors had black lettered stenciling that identified rooms for janitorial and laundry services. The smells of disinfectants reminded him of the stench from the marshes around the Meadowlands. Hampers lined the hall, ready to have their contents processed in large vats. Next was the kitchen where huge women stirred cauldrons of bubbling, gruel-like substances

65

with spoons large enough to propel canoes.

Unlike the other doors with their opaque glass and black letters, Room B114 was solid wood. "Records Office." He knocked but heard no response. The knob yielded easily to a scant turn. The barren room was separated by a high counter that ran across its width, keeping anyone who might want information at a comfortable distance.

He was greeted by a broad picket-fence smile attached to the full face of a woman who was humming while she sorted number-coded Manila charts. Phillip noticed a large chrome-framed picture depicting the same woman beaming at a tall, gawky boy and a neatly dressed girl.

"Excuse me . . . ," Phillip glanced at the laminated hospital identification badge that swung from her breast pocket, ". . . uh, Miss Bathgate, I wonder if you could help me? My name's Phillip Hunter and I was born here on March 21, 1975."

"Yes . . ." she said, with a Jamaican lilt.

"There seems to be a question as to who my parents are. I was hoping I'd be able to check the records."

"Good Lord, are you adopted, child?"

"No . . . that's not it." He studied her eyes.

"Then what was it?"

"I was wondering if . . . if you. . . ."

"Get on with it, boy. Can't you see that pile of charts I got to put away?"

He rocked from foot-to-foot. "Okay, here goes. I was switched in the nursery."

"You was what?"

"Switched in the nursery . . . with another baby. I've got papers here to prove it," he said, and placed the lab results from the Essex County Blood Center and a letter from Dr.

Novick on the counter top. "It's pretty simple: my parents took home the wrong kid."

She reached for glasses tied to a string around her neck. She read the papers. Finished, she took them off.

"Every once in a while, a kid comes in here claiming they was adopted. Usually, it's because their brother or sister teased them. I thought that was your problem." She reread the documents then handed them back.

"Believe me, I wish someone was teasing me," he said.

"Lordy, you've got quite a problem! My, my! Years ago, a similar thing happened in this hospital. But the parents found out after two weeks. So, Phillip Hunter, what now? What can I do for you?"

"I was hoping you would give me the list of babies born the same week I was so I could find my natural parents."

"I wish I could, but I can't."

"Can anyone?"

"The hospital administrator can authorize something like that, but he's away until Monday. I'll tell you what I'm going to do," she said. "I'll arrange a meeting with you and the administrator first thing Monday morning. How's that?"

"That's great," he said. "I'll be here early."

"I'll bet you will."

Empty-handed, Phillip paid the garage attendant and pulled out of the lot. He made a quick left and then the first right and found Weequahic Avenue, the street his father lived on as a boy. He had never been there before but knew where it was. Though Brad had talked about his childhood house often, it never occurred to Phillip the area would be run-down. It wasn't a slum, but he wouldn't trade residences with anyone on the block.

The houses were close together, with front yards not more than thirty feet wide, and in a pinch, you could pass something to your neighbor by leaning through a window. Shades had to be pulled down for privacy, and telephone conversations were neighborly events.

Patches of stucco had flaked off most of the houses and the raw cement underneath had been painted so many times that it, too, was flaking off. Thick slabs of cement held the brick stoops together. Each house had a narrow cement driveway that led to an unattached, one-car garage in the rear. There was more cement about the houses than grass. Cement sidewalks, found on either side of the street, were cracked by the roots of old maple trees in front of every house. Weeds grew through the cracks like cowlicks—unmanageable and unwanted.

He found number 217. In front of it, two black girls jumped rope at the same time. Not one rope but two! Taller, older girls were at either end, turning them in opposite directions. A rhythm had been found and the younger girls jumped effortlessly, avoiding being snagged at their ankles. His father had once described this as "doing the Double-Dutch." No one in the suburbs could do that!

The narrowness of the street closed in on him, and Phillip felt he needed to leave. A few days earlier he had no need to peep into his father's past, no craving to fix his own identity. But now, a plucked hair and a vial of blood later, his world was turned upside down. Did he really want to know who his biological parents were? And why was he parked on a street in Newark, New Jersey, whisking tears from his cheeks with the back of his hand?

♥♥

8

"**B**id 'em like you have 'em, partner," said Rick Sturnweiss. Brad fanned his cards and arranged them so the picture cards led each suit. He licked his lips when he counted his points.

"Trish, have you finished shopping for the trip?" asked Susan.

"One club," said Brad.

"Pass. I'm almost done. A few odds and ends left. That's all. Then Algarve, here I come," she answered.

"One heart," Rick bid. "I hear the water's a lot colder than the Caribbean."

"Pass. Vivian Gersten told me the beaches are topless. Rick, you get blinders." Susan mockingly covered his eyes.

"Whoa! I'll get the kind horses wear; you know the one's that help you see straight ahead."

"Very funny."

"Two spades," answered Brad.

"Way to go, partner."

"Hey, Rick. What's with the table talk?" Trish asked.

"Sorry, Trish. It's just that Brad and I never get good hands. We've played every Friday night since Ford was president and you girls get all the cards. You can't blame me for getting excited, can you?"

"You don't have to be obnoxious about it. Pass."

"Three hearts."

"Pass."

"Six hearts."

"Brad, I hate when you do that."

"Do what, Trish? You're jealous we have points for a change."

"When will you learn? Every time you and Rick get some points, you push the bidding without exploring which suit to be in. You end up too high without establishing your suit. I'm tired of setting your contracts."

"You should be tickled pink we let you win each week."

"You don't let us win. The ladies are better players. When you get a good hand, you blow it with those ridiculous bids."

"Eh, sometimes you're right, but in a few minutes I'm going to make this small slam. Then you'll eat your words. Lead a card."

Trish led the two of spades and Rick placed his cards on the table, the trump to his right. Brad counted the winning tricks in his head and realized Trish was right—he needed two finesses to make the contract. Once on the board, he end-played Sue with the king of diamonds. She let it go, choosing to save her ace for later. Bingo! He dropped his lone diamond loser. Back in his hand, he played his jack of clubs through Trish. She went up with queen and he overtook the trick with the king. All the tricks were now his.

"See that, Trish. You have very little faith in your husband. He even made an over trick."

"Rick, your friend bids wildly and jumps the gun too often for my taste. It's hard to trust his common sense when he acts so impulsively."

"But it's only a game, Trish."

"Rick," she said, "bridge is like life: play it recklessly and you'll end up with a losing hand when all the cards are counted."

Brad and Rick's glory was short-lived; the wives added more points to their on-going score. Their tally competed with the national debt.

After the Sturnweisses left, Brad was reading in the den when the boys came home.

"How was the movie?"

"Great, if you like Sly dangling from a wooden bridge," Ron said. "He did use two syllable words this time."

"Bull! You loved it," said Todd.

"Not. I said I appreciated it; lately, I'm into more intellectual movies. You know, French subtitles. *Cinema verité.*"

"The only intellectual movie you understand is one with naked women."

"Todd, that's enough. Why don't you guys go to bed."

"C'mon, Dad, it's the weekend. There's no school tomorrow."

"It's past midnight. Then you and Todd get ready. How 'bout reading a book *not* on a school list?"

"Daaaaaad," they chorused.

"Just kidding, just kidding. I lost my mind for a second. That's what happens when you get old. Good night, fellas."

Todd and Ron kissed Brad on the cheek. Phillip lingered.

"Aren't you tired, Phil?"

"Nope. There's something I have to tell you."

"Is it about the blood tests?" Phillip nodded. "What about them?" Brad asked.

"I did fine this morning, Dad. Really. But now, I'm scared and confused. I'm not sure how I'm supposed to act around you or even what I'm supposed to say. I thought I was so cool telling you I could handle it. But I guess I'm not."

"I'm having the same problem. All day, I stopped in mid-sentence and imagined what you might be doing at that moment. Sometimes bits and pieces of things you said and did as a kid flashed through my mind. It was like playing old reruns in my head . . . in slow motion.

"That's not what's happening to me. My problem is that when I look in the mirror, I don't know who's looking back. It's my reflection all right, but it's not me. My body feels strange to me, like someone has taken my place."

"Where were you this afternoon?" Brad asked.

"Why?"

"I called the lab to see how you were doing and Frank said you had left. Where'd you go?"

"You really want to know? To the Beth."

"The Beth? You went to Beth Israel Hospital? What in God's name for?"

"At first, I didn't realize that's where I was headed. I was on my way home, and then all of a sudden, I found myself driving to Newark, like something pulled me there. Then I knew. I had to find them."

Brad winced.

"Did you?"

"No. The woman at the records office was real nice. She said I had to come back Monday—to see the hospital administrator."

"Jeez, and to think I was worried about you."

In 1985, Phillip was ten when Brad took him on a trip to the Amazon with the Audubon Society. They had been stuck in the airport for six hours, along with twenty-five other passengers who gazed at print, lolled in their seats, and wearily fanned their faces, waiting for the broken plane to be fixed. When Phillip wearied of swatting large green flies dubbed "bombardiers," Brad told him it was all right to

inspect the terminal. Wilted and hungry, the stranded bird-
ers' lethargy soon changed to fear.

Armed soldiers cordoned off the lounge without an expla-
nation and herded all the men into the bathroom. Demand-
ing they strip, the jungle explorers were poked and prodded
in every private place. Finding no drugs, they dressed and
were marched through the terminal and onto a waiting bus.
Phillip was nowhere to be seen.

The rattletrap bus spewed a wake of putrid smoke, scuttling
Brad and the others to a police station. To Brad's shock,
Phillip was drinking a Coke while teaching a soldier how to
use his hand-held game of Donkey-Kong.

"Hi, Dad! What took you so long?" Phillip asked.

"Are you all right?"

Brad didn't answer.

"Dad?" Phillip touched his shoulder. "Dad?"

"Uh, what?"

"What were you thinking about? You zoned out."

"Sorry, Phillip, I was . . . I'm going with you Monday.
You're going to need all the help you can get."

"Dad, you don't have to bother. I mean you've got
work and. . . ."

"It's more than that, Phillip. I want to be there for you
. . . as well as for me. Did you stop to think that your mother
and I have another . . . well, we've given birth to. . . ."

"Dad? I'm scared."

"So am I, Phillip."

For the first time since Frank rang their doorbell, a deep
sleep engulfed Brad. He slept fitfully through the night. In
the morning, the aroma of freshly brewed coffee teased his
nostrils. Suspended in a hazy twilight, he covered his head,

wishing to doze more, but he had reached the irreversible edge of consciousness.

"Hi!" Brad filled a mug with steaming coffee. He blew on the surface. Trish wore a white terry-cloth robe.

"Something's wrong. I can feel it," she said.

Brad walked to the opposite end of the kitchen table, started to speak, and then thought otherwise. He sat down.

"Brad, what is it?"

"Phillip went to Beth."

"Oh shit! You said he took it like it was no big deal. You told me it was finally over." She slumped. "This is turning into my worst nightmare. Phillip wants to find his biological parents. Right? That's it, isn't it?"

"He tried to get the names of the babies who were in the nursery with him. And what I said was that he took it like I expected."

"I hope the idiots knew enough not to tell him."

"They couldn't, at least not yet."

"What do you mean 'not yet'? Brad, make sure he never gets those names. There's no reason for him to have them."

"What are you doing?" Brad asked.

A match flared. "Lighting a cigarette. What does it look like?" White gusts swirled from her dejected lips. "This better be over soon. That's all I can tell you."

Brad slid into the chair opposite her.

"Pull yourself together, this is not as bad as it seems. The odds of Phillip finding them are close to nil. This way, I get to help him. He won't feel abandoned, and the whole thing will die down before you know it. What's the harm in helping him?"

She lit another cigarette with the red ember.

"We'll lose him, that's all."

Rankled, he wagged his finger.

"Mark my words, Trish, we'll lose him if he doesn't get

those names. That's why I'm going to help. He's only a boy. He's curious about where he comes from. I don't blame him. So am I . . . I mean, curious about our son."

"Christ, there you go again. Phillip's our son! What in God's name are you trying to prove? That you're a dutiful goody-goody bent on wrecking this family."

She stubbed out the cigarette.

"Keep your voice down. The boys are sleeping." He listened for footsteps. "I'm not trying to do anything but help him. He needs to know who his parents are."

"*We* are his parents," she snarled with bared enamel.

"Not really, Trish. True, we raised him and loved him like a son. . . ."

She hurled the half-empty pack at him; cigarettes scattered as it tumbled to the floor.

"You're certifiable. What do I have to do to make you stop this madness? You're wrecking our family! Christ, our lives used to be tolerable, at least we functioned day-to-day. It's been no bed of roses, but shit, Brad, no one's got that. Then Frank plays genetic super-sleuth and for the first time in his life, turns into Honest Abe. The bastard should've left the mysteries of DNA to Watson and Crick."

Trish snorted. Her head moved back and forth, cobra-like. The muscles in her jaw bulged. Her hands opened and closed. Her lips quivered. Another match sparked.

Brad reached to place his hand on her shoulder; she batted it away.

"Don't you dare touch me. Don't ever touch me again. I can't trust you. . . ."

She hiccupped.

"Shit." Her body heaved with each lancing spasm.

"Here." He handed her a teaspoonful of sugar.

"That never works."

"Works for me all the time. Try it." She gulped the spoonful of white granules; her face and lips wrinkled at the sweetness. Trish waited for the next pang—it never came.

"Trish?" Trish grabbed Brad's hand, and, as she stood, he coaxed her into him. She didn't resist. He tasted her salty tears.

"Brad, when I met you, getting into a relationship was the furthest thing from my mind. I didn't trust men, but you were different. You were strong and decisive, yet gentle and sweet when I needed you to be. We worked well together. What went wrong? Where'd it all go?"

He nuzzled her hair.

"Baby, baby, can't you see it's all still the same. I love you. Everything I do is for you and the kids."

"I can't stand when they get like that. Christ, it drives me crazy. They must think we're still little kids and can't hear them," said Ron.

"Yeah, they've been doing it a lot lately. It scares me," Todd said.

Todd and Ron were seated between the compact disc cases and a dozen or so back issues of *Sporting News,* which were strewn over Phillip's extra twin bed. The two-tone beige wallpaper was plastered with posters of Patrick Ewing, Michael Jordan, Rickey Henderson, Cal Ripken, Dwight Gooden, and Joe Montana, plus yellowed newspaper clippings of the 1986 Mets.

"You know how parents get when the kids aren't in the room," said Phillip.

"I wish they wouldn't do it," said Ron.

"They've got an excuse this time," said Phillip.

"How come they're screaming?" Todd asked idly.

Phillip raised his hand hesitantly.

"Uh, it's about me."

"I'm glad it's not me this time." Ron broke into a leprechaun smile.

"Is Gillian pregnant?"

"Todd, you've been going to too many health classes."

"Then what gives?"

"Dad must've told Mom he's going with me to Beth Israel Hospital on Monday morning."

Ron lunged across the bed and seized Phillip's shoulders. Worried eyes mirrored Ron's fears.

"Relax, I'm not sick. Damn, I could deal with that. The problem is . . . I found out that Mom and Dad are not my parents. Frank showed me this experiment and. . . ."

"Of course they're our parents. Who else's are they?" Todd asked.

"Yours."

"Ours?"

"Yours. It seems they took the wrong baby home from the hospital. Your brother went with my parents."

"But you're our brother."

"I still am, Ron. That'll never change."

"So what's the problem?" Ron asked.

"Dad said he would help me. We're going to get the list of babies born the same week I was. If we do, then we can track down my biological parents."

"Why's Mom making such a fuss?" Todd asked.

"She thinks she's losing a son."

"That's ridiculous," Ron said.

"I know it, but she doesn't. She needs time to get used to this."

"You gotta admit it's kind of mind-blowing to find out your son's not your son," Ron said.

"Phil, are you still my brother?" Todd asked.

Phillip wrapped his arms around him.

"You dummy, of course I'm still your brother. Who else would put up with you?"

Phillip stuck his fist, waist high, in front of them. Todd put his hand on top of Phillip's and Ron covered Todd's. They repeated the act until their six hands were a totem pole.

"Todd . . . Ron . . . don't ever forget, we're Hunters forever."

"Hunters forever."

9

❦❦

"I didn't think there'd be this much traffic on Monday morning. Hey, quit flicking the stations. What're you looking for?" Brad asked. Phillip pushed the scan button to WFAN.

"How can you live without Imus? He's the best."

They parked on the lower level across from the brick sanctuary; Phillip scooted up the stone stairs by threes, then waited for Brad. Phillip referred to Ms. Bathgate's instructions and located Room A20 beyond the information desk. There was no one to greet them so they sat on the connected plastic chairs, which looked like an eight-legged orange glowworm.

Phillip drummed his fingers on the cheap, brown formica table and tapped his foot on the worn linoleum floor. The thudding and cracking sounds filled the room.

"Please stop that, it's annoying."

"Sorry, Dad."

Except for the molded chairs, the rickety table and the secretary's desk, there was no furniture in the hospital administrator's office. Phillip wondered where the secretary was.

"Stop it! You're shaking the seats," Brad said as he put his hand on Phillip's bouncing leg. "Where did you get such a disgusting habit?"

"From you. You told me you used to do it."

"I told you that because I wanted you to stop."

"Not today. I'm too nervous."

From the inner office, they heard a deep, booming voice express displeasure at a vendor whose supplies did not meet hospital specifications. Phillip tried to picture the administrator, whose name, Ezekial U. Johnson, was engraved on a sign on the office door. Phillip imagined he would not be very tall, have a paunchy stomach, and would be wearing Coke bottle glasses. His short hair would make him appear scholarly, and he'd be wearing a wrinkled faded blue seersucker suit. Phillip couldn't have been further off!

The beanpole secretary with teased hair returned to her desk with a can of soda and a candy bar. The light on the phone line disappeared, indicating that the beleaguered vendor had been dismissed. The intercom crackled a static-filled command.

She gulped the last bite of candy, licking chocolate flakes from her lips. "Mr. Johnson'll see you now. Through that door," she said while pointing.

The office was small. Every square inch was covered with manuals, books and custom-bound leather ledgers. Ezekial Johnson stood to greet them, dwarfing his desk and the two chairs in front by what seemed like miles. Phillip gulped. The man was massive! He might have played defensive end or power forward when he was younger. He immediately frightened Phillip, who was thankful his father was with him.

Size aside, with prominent cheekbones and slightly flared nostrils, and with lips that were thin and upturned, the administrator was ruggedly handsome. Mr. Johnson reminded Phillip of Sidney Poitier, except for his massive Afro, which was laced with patches of silver. He wore a flowery deep orange dashiki, symbolic of a Masai warrior. Brawny arms greeted them.

"What can I do for you fellas."

Brad cleared his throat. "Thank you for seeing us, Mr. Johnson. We hope you can help us."

Brad explained how Frank Bellman had come to question Phillip's parentage by dint of viewing his hair sample through a microscope. When he had finished, Brad handed him copies of the lab results, a letter from Dr. Novick, and Phillip's original birth certificate.

The big man read the papers.

"What would you have me do, Mr. Hunter?"

"I . . . that is we, hoped you'd give us a list of the babies in the nursery with Phillip. We would take it from there."

"I see," he said, in a honeyed baritone. "Off the record, I want to say how sorry I am that this happened." He looked from Brad to Phillip. "This is one of those administrative nightmares you pray never happens. A couple of years ago, there was a story in the papers about a baby who'd been sick from the time she left the hospital. The parents spent their life savings caring for her. Finally, she needed a heart and lung transplant, and that's when they found her blood type didn't match either parent."

"Didn't she die?" Phillip asked.

"That's the one. They were the only white babies in the hospital at the time, which makes it pretty hard to understand how such a mistake was made. I heard the babies were deliberately switched because the parents of the sick child figured the other family knew how to care for it since they had six or seven children already. They wanted a healthy one."

"NBC made that into a movie. They never mentioned anything about intentionally switching the babies."

"It was never proved. But my cousin knows the head nurse in that hospital. It seems the woman had a sick child of her own and needed the money. I'm sure she thought no one would ever catch on. You know how all white babies with blond hair look the same." The creases in the corners of his eyes turned up as he smiled broadly showing a block of teeth.

"Come to think of it, I could never identify my baby through the nursery window without reading the name on the bassinet. I never bothered looking at the babies wrapped in pink. Assumed they were girls. But who knows now?"

"You realize, Mr. Hunter, that no one deliberately switched Phillip."

"I didn't say it was deliberate. All we want is for you to help us. Will you?"

Mr. Johnson placed his elbows on the desk. His palms faced each other. Their eyes were glued to two sets of pink fingertips that rapidly tapped together—ten fingers barely touching, yet radiating strength. His voice broke their trance.

"When Ms. Bathgate informed me of this on Friday, I got in touch with our legal counsel. It seems our lawyers are concerned about . . . well, let's just say we would like to avoid any unpleasantness that might arise from a situation like this."

"What are you getting at, Mr. Johnson?" Brad asked.

"This . . ." he said and handed each of them a typed letter that had been on his desk.

"What are they?"

"Releases, Mr. Hunter."

"Why do we need them?"

"What are they, Dad?"

"They protect the hospital, Phillip," Mr. Johnson said. "The hospital could be blamed for this unfortunate incident even though we deny having any direct responsibility. These papers say you relinquish the right to sue Beth Israel Hospital or anyone associated with it, for this. . . ."

"Unfortunate incident," Phillip said, mimickingly.

"That's right. The bottom line is that we're awfully sorry it happened and we do want to help you. But we need to protect ourselves. You can see that, can't you?"

"Our only concern is to find Phillip's biological parents. We're not looking to cause any problems or change anyone's life."

"That sounds sensible enough." Ezekial Johnson handed them a black pen with a gold tip. He took the signed papers and slipped them in a folder, placing them in a locked drawer. Then, he buzzed for his secretary.

"Yolanda, please take Mr. Hunter and Phillip to the records office."

"Yes, sir. This way please," she said, holding the wooden door with her skinny arms.

"It might take some time. The microfilm is buried under stacks of cartons. But if any one can find it, Melita Bathgate can."

"Yeah, she's nice," Phillip said.

"Anytime." The three men shook hands.

Fortunately for them, Melita Bathgate was an efficient record keeper. Twenty minutes was all she needed to find the small, metallic cans that held the names they sought.

"Phillip, do you know. . . ."

"I sure do, Ms. Bathgate," he said, grabbing them. Phillip had spotted the microfilm machine in the corner while they had waited. It was buried under an avalanche of papers and files. He vaulted over the counter and cleared away the papers.

"The average maternity stay when you were born was four days," she told him. "Babies were admitted by their last name, so look for admissions like *Boy Smith, Girl Jones,* and so on."

"Got it," Phillip said, blowing the dust away from the screen. He threaded the first roll of film onto the sprockets and scrolled the microfiche until he found his birth date. Brad wrote as Phillip called out the names of every baby born three days before or after he was. They handed the list to Ms. Bathgate who took an hour before she returned from the file room, carrying a box of charts.

"Thanks for your help." Brad slipped her $20 as Phillip took the carton.

"You're very welcome. You can use the table in the corner."

Pulling two wooden chairs in front of the table, they split the pile of charts in half. Girls eliminated, they compiled a list of every reasonable prospect. Names like *Wang* and *Fong* or *Singh* were not considered. Brad checked the discarded files one last time, certain they didn't overlook any possibilities.

"I guess that does it," Phillip said, looking at the list. "Thank you very much."

"May the good Lord give you strength and guidance," she said, crossing herself as they left.

Brad and Phillip followed the blue line to the elevator, anxious to leave the catacombs of the hospital. Walking stride for stride, they passed the information desk, with the same old man giving directions to anyone with the patience to listen. The bright sunlight hurt their eyes but the fresh air came as a relief after being in the hospital basement.

"Hungry?" Brad asked. It was after two o'clock.

"Famished. How 'bout Don's?" Phillip was always ready to go to Livingston's hamburger haven.

"Don's it is."

They paid the parking fee. Phillip held the list of names in his hand, wondering if they would really find his biological parents. He started to unfold the paper. "Save it for the restaurant," Brad said. Phillip hesitated and put it in his shirt pocket. "Besides, I have to do something." That something was the same thing his son had done three days earlier. They turned right on Weequahic Avenue, and traveled back to 1958.

Every night during the summer, the kids on the block congregated in front of Brad's house to play running bases or ring-a-lievo. When they played hide-and-seek, they used the big maple tree for "home base." The girls played in the nighttime games, but during the day, they were excluded from stoop ball or stick ball. When no one else was around, Brad played box baseball with Maureen Rogers, and always won. The boys looked at girls differently when they came around with packages of baseball cards. Then, they were invited to join their games. The girls rarely knocked down a "leaner" or got the knack of "star toppers" and in minutes, ownership of the cards changed hands.

Each night they played until their shirts were sticky with sweat and their faces were covered with dirt. Sometimes they would get empty pickle jars and catch fireflies. Billy Masterson had the pointed screwdriver everyone used to punch air holes through the metal lids. But no matter what care they took, the fireflies never lived more than a day.

The cement driveway ended in front of the wooden garage, above which his father had nailed a homemade plywood backboard. The strings were forever breaking from the orange-painted basket. When the backboard warped, only Brad knew where every soft spot was. He needed that advantage because most of the kids were better than him. In the winter, they cleared the snow away, though Brad was afraid the ball would freeze and shatter when it hit the cement.

There was a cherry tree in the tiny backyard. The cherries

were eye-crunching sour but he would eat them until he got
a bellyache. Brad would sit on his favorite branch high up
in the tree, higher than the garage and daydream about all
the things boys his age daydreamed about.

The maple tree was no longer in front of the house and
the outline of the backboard could barely be seen on the
garage. This wasn't the house he remembered, only the
number was the same. He pressed down on the accelerator,
needing to get away, to safeguard his childhood memories
and keep things the way they were.

At Don's, they wolfed down the hamburgers in a matter
of seconds. Phillip pressed his fingers onto the tiny crumbs
in the basket and licked the remnants of the onion rings until
there was nothing left. Pushing their plates away, Phillip
spread the paper in front of them while their chests
pounded.

Which ones were his parents? Which one was his son?

They looked at the list.

> March 18, 1975
> Baby Wilson—boy
> Margaret and Peter Wilson
> 1745 Fairview Avenue
> Kearney, New Jersey
>
> March 20, 1975
> Robert Eliot Schwartz
> Shirley and Bernard Schwartz
> 17 Montana Drive
> South Orange, New Jersey
>
> March 20, 1975
> Baby Lantelli—boy
> Maria and Anthony Lantelli
> 426 Heritage Lane
> Milburn, New Jersey

March 21, 1975
Winfield Arlen Jones, III
Thelma and Winfield Jones, Jr.
Laurel Manor Road
Mt. Laurel, New Jersey

March 21, 1975
Ari Kenneth Ruderman
Esther and Morris Ruderman
232 Goldsmith Avenue
Newark, New Jersey

March 21, 1975
Phillip Langley Hunter
Patricia and Bradley Hunter
42 Coddington Terrace
Livingston, New Jersey

March 22, 1975
Baby Manning—boy
Sally and Thomas Manning
2385 Oakridge Circle
Hillside, New Jersey

March 23, 1975
Joshua Steven Baines
Ellen and Jonathan Baines
189 Vesper Lane
West Orange, New Jersey

"Let's eliminate the first and last names," Brad said. "We have to assume no one would confuse babies who were three days younger or older than each other. Wilson and Baines go. If we strike out, we can come back to them."

"Sounds okay."

"That leaves five names: Schwartz, Lantelli, Jones, Ruderman, and Manning." Brad looked at his son. Phillip had tried to clear his throat but gagged. Brad slapped him on the back. "Hey, are you all right?"

He wiped his nose with the napkin. "I don't know, this is getting weird. This list . . . the names . . . it's so real."

"Listen, we don't. . . ."

"I'm scared, Dad, but I want to go through with it. I need to know who they are."

"We might not be able to find them after all this time, you know."

Brad paid the check as Phillip walked ahead. A poem he had memorized years earlier kept running through his head:

> *I shall be telling this with a sigh*
> *Somewhere ages and ages hence:*
> *Two roads diverged in a wood, and I—*
> *I took the one less traveled by,*
> *And that has made all the difference.*

✿✿

10

"G' morning, Tommy. Anything important happen yesterday?" Brad never returned to work the day before. After his late lunch with Phillip, he picked up Trish at her office and they went to a movie and then to dinner.

"Yeah, Boss. Joe called. Said to tell you the catalogues are finished. He's Fed-Exing one for you to see. The mailing company picked them up from the binder. They'll be labeled and sorted by zip code by the end of the day."

"Great! I knew Joe would come through. We've got lots of inventory we have to sell." He waved his hand at the bins of goods.

"It's gonna be a winner, Boss. Replacing the old-style music boxes with microchips was pure genius. You'll be king of the Christmas gifts."

"I hope you're right, Tommy."

"Of course I'm right, Boss, 'cause you always know what to do."

Brad wondered. Had he been right helping Phillip search for his parents? He wished he had as much faith in himself as Tommy did.

About the same time, Phillip walked into Frank's office.

"Did you guys survive without me?"

Frank put his pipe down. "Barely. Why don't you give up the idea of being a vet? We could use you here."

"And work with Mr. Soo? No, thanks." Everyone knew the lab technician was the easiest person in the world to get along with, though he was difficult to understand when he became excited.

"Seriously, Phillip, how are you holding up? Is there anything I can do to help?"

"I'm fine, thanks for asking." Frank stuck his right thumb up in the air and Phillip returned the signal.

"I'm glad, because . . . well, I've been feeling way down about what I did."

"I told you before, you didn't do anything."

"I know, but I can't help feeling I've thrown you to the lions."

"Uh, couldn't you pick a different image? Dad found the address of the first family; we're going there this afternoon."

Phillip got to Brad's place by two.

"You're early," said Brad. His son shrugged. "Guess I would be, too. We got lucky with this one. They're at the same address and it's twenty minutes from here."

A woman, about forty, answered the door. She wore a hot pink and green leotard, and her black-dyed hair was pulled back with matching scarf. Rings of moisture circled her neck and arms. She wiped her face with a hand towel.

"Yes?"

"Pardon me, is this the Schwartz's residence?"

"Yes, it is. May I help you?" she asked, drying her neck.

"I hope so. I'm Brad Hunter and this is my son, Phillip." With pursed lips, she waited for Brad to continue. "Actually, I don't know where to begin. This whole thing is so unbelievable."

Her hand grabbed the door.

"I'm not interested in whatever it is you're selling."

"Be patient, Mrs. Schwartz. This isn't easy for me. The truth of the matter is your son, Robert . . . your son's name is Robert, isn't it?" She nodded. "Well, Robert and Phillip were born the same week at the Beth, in 1975."

"So?"

"You're not going to believe this." He took a breath. "Recently we found out that Phillip isn't . . . well . . . our biological son. My wife and I took home the wrong boy from the hospital."

"That's impossible."

"We thought so, too. But it happened. We found our blood types don't match, so we had our DNA compared. That didn't match either. So now we're searching for the other family. I mean, Phillip and I . . . well, we want to find his real parents."

"But what do you want from me?" She inched back and started to close the door.

"We were hoping you'd be understanding and tell us your son's blood type. After all, he might not be yours."

"You're nuts! You had me going there for a minute. You ring my doorbell and claim my son might belong to you? And you bring a kid to make it believable! What kind of scam are you running, mister?"

As Phillip put his foot in the way of the closing door, Brad saw the woman reach for an alarm button. Brad tugged on his son's arm and pulled him away.

They turned and began to leave as she opened up the door a crack.

"Phillip? That's your name? Is this on the level?"

"Yes, ma'am, it is. We don't mean you any harm. I'm just trying to find my natural parents, that's all." He felt naked under her gaze. "Mrs. Schwartz?"

"Yes?"

"What's Robert's blood type?"

"Blood type? You look sweet, kid, but you're both crazy!" She slammed the door. Brad reached to push the doorbell but Phillip took his hand.

"Let's go, Dad. This isn't the way to do it." They walked down the gray flagstone path. Phillip looked back and saw a curtain in the living room move.

"Wow! Can you believe that lady? I sure hope she isn't my mother."

"Amen to that! Imagine what her son must be like. But look at it from her point of view: two people show up claiming she may have raised the wrong son for eighteen years. How *should* she act?"

"How did you feel when Frank did that to you?"

"Differently than Mrs. Schwartz did. Remember, I *knew* Frank. It was the most preposterous thing I had ever heard, but I listened because he's my brother-in-law. Besides, he's a scientist."

"But how did you feel?"

"Like I was punched in the stomach."

They got in the car. Brad looked at his watch. "Let's go to my office. While I'm working, you can use the phone book to try to find the others."

"Okay."

They pulled into the narrow driveway of the Ceram-Electric Mold Company.

"Why did you do it, Dad?"

"Do what, Phil?"

"Tell me about it. I might never have found out."

"Wait a second. You were the one who was checking our blood types, not me. You asked Frank for help. Remember?"

"But he covered it up so smoothly. I didn't give it much thought until. . . ."

"Until what?"

"Until everyone started behaving strangely."

"Phillip, we didn't know what to do. What if you needed a transfusion or an organ transplant one day. That's when you would've found out. What was I going to tell you? I didn't know about it?"

"No, you're right. I guess I'm glad you told me. It means a lot that you're helping me. I couldn't have faced Mrs. Schwartz alone, but, I hope the others are more understanding."

"So do I. Look Phillip, we're in this together. You must be so confused, I know I am. Can you keep a secret? I'm curious to see what my biological son looks like. Guess curiosity has gotten to both of us."

"Let's hope that curiosity treats us better than it did the cat," Phillip said.

"But cats have nine lives!" Brad slapped his son's outstretched palm.

Trish was peeling vegetables when Brad and Phillip entered the kitchen. She tipped her head so Brad could give her a kiss. They waited for her to ask how they made out but she continued preparing the salad.

"Don't you want to know what happened?" Brad asked.

"Not particularly."

"Well, I'm glad you're my mother, Mom. Mrs. Schwartz wasn't anywhere near as nice as you."

"That's nice. Dinner will be ready in ten minutes. Why don't you get washed up."

Dinner had been over for an hour when Brad asked Trish to join him for a stroll. They walked up the hill at the end of their block without a word between them. At the top, he turned.

Trish lit a cigarette.

"Why are you behaving this way?" he asked. "And when

are you going to stop that disgusting habit?"

"When you give up this ridiculous search," she answered cooly.

"But we've always supported each other. I have to do this."

"Am I supposed to approve of my husband trying to find my son's biological parents? Well, I don't approve." Trish dragged deeply. "I may be your wife but that doesn't give you license to do what you want, and ignore me. We've gone over it a thousand times and I still don't get it. Why do you need to pursue this? Leave well enough alone."

"Because I have to find out who our son is. I need to see what he looks like, hear him speak. Don't you have these same feelings?"

"Not in the slightest. The only feelings I have are frustration and hurt. I pray you come to your senses and end this foolishness before it's too late."

"Before what's too late?"

"It's what I've said all along, if you continue to search for this so-called son of ours, I know our lives will change. We'll lose Phillip."

"C'mon, Trish. Don't be like that. You know I love you."

She lowered her shoulders. "If you really love me, you'd stop this lunacy. You know you could."

"I can't."

"That's bullshit, Brad. I know you. You can do anything you set your mind to. You always have. So where do you come off telling me you can't stop yourself?" She bit her lower lip. "The sad thing is that you're acting so much like my father used to, except *you're* not drunk. At least he had an excuse when he became irrational. What's yours?"

"Trish, I love you."

"That's what my father said every time the cops brought him home so plastered he couldn't remember where he lived. That's what he said when my mother had a black eye. And that's what he said when he. . . ."

Trish spun from his clutches and stormed down the hill, leaving Brad to wonder if he was making a terrible mistake.

11

❧❧

The phone book yielded no other leads. At Brad's suggestion, they went to the last known address of the next family on the list.

"Mrs. Lantelli?" Brad asked.

"No. She used to live here. We bought the house from the Lantellis eight years ago." The woman appeared to be in her sixties. She had white hair held back by a sheer net, and her gold wire-rimmed glasses made her look like a model for Norman Rockwell. "May I help you? I'm Jean Harnell." She smiled at Phillip as if the next thing she'd do was offer him milk and cookies.

"Maybe you can, Mrs. Harnell. Do you know where the Lantellis moved to? This is sort of important."

"When we bought this place, they were building a house up the hill." She pointed to where they had just come from.

"Livingston?" Phillip asked.

"No, Short Hills. They wanted to stay in town so their son could finish school here." At the mention of "their son," Phillip's heart beat faster.

Brad took over. "Mrs. Harnell, do you happen to know where in Short Hills?"

"Not exactly. But I do remember them saying it was close to something called the Taj Mahal. Does that help you, Mr . . . Mr . . . ?"

"Oh, I'm terribly sorry. My name is Brad Hunter and this is Phillip. And yes, you've been a big help. Thank you."

They returned to Brad's Volvo.

"I think I've seen the house," Phillip said.

"Of course you have. Every Christmas, I piled you, Ron and Todd in my old Caprice station wagon, and we drove through Livingston, Milburn, and Short Hills looking at the decorations. We passed the Taj Mahal many times."

"Are we going there, now?"

"You bet."

After passing the Paper Mill Playhouse, Brad took a shortcut down a winding road lined with ancient oak and poplar trees so tall and broad that their intertwining branches formed a tunnel of green that blocked the sunlight. On either side they could see white houses with slate roofs and red horse stables with fenced in yards. The road emerged to the bustle of South Orange Avenue, the same steep incline Phillip had used to get to the deer sanctuary a few days earlier. Brad turned left at the top of the hill and entered a section of Milburn called Newstead.

The homes were not built on lots but were part of the land. The mostly wooden and glass structures emerged from the earth as if the houses were planted and allowed to grow according to nature's whims. Not a blade of grass was too long and the shrubs were perfectly manicured. The care of these five-, six-, and ten-thousand-square-foot mansions was entrusted to landscapers, not gardeners.

Shortly, they found the Taj Mahal, a white domed building that faithfully called to mind its namesake. But there were no clues as to the whereabouts of the Lantellis.

97

They were about to give up when Phillip saw it, "There it is," he said.

"Good going."

"Why were you so sure we'd find it?"

"Because Italians build houses out of brick and most of these are modern, trimmed with wood, glass, and different types of stone facings."

They looked at the house. In spite of the curtains being partially open, it had that feeling of stillness, like no one was home.

"Well?" Brad asked.

"I'm scared," his son replied.

They approached the double doors slowly. The cream-colored brick house was built like a fortress. Only gun holes were missing, and the tiny garage windows were reminiscent of them.

Brad hit the large gold knocker twice. Nothing. He did it again and the sound reverberated through the house. Phillip found the doorbell button and pushed it. An eight-chime bell rang, emitting church-like tones. Phillip listened for the sound of a hunchback dragging his lame leg along the marble floor who would open the door and get his Master. But no such sounds came.

"We'll try tomorrow, Phil."

"I sure hope they aren't on vacation. This stuff is getting to me."

"Me, too."

Walking to their car, Phillip saw the lucite backboard mounted to a steel pole in the driveway. How did he miss it before? If circumstances had been different, would he have been playing here for the last eight years?

Promising to return the next day, they headed home.

They turned onto their block to see Todd and Ron playing one-on-one basketball. Brad and Phillip challenged them and, for a while, kept it respectable. Todd and Ron won and couldn't convince the losers to a rematch. Gasping for air and clutching his chest, Brad paid his debt for being out of shape.

At dinner, Ron turned to Phillip, "How's the search coming?"

Before Phillip had a chance to respond, Trish got up and left the room. Brad started after her but returned to his seat, thinking she would eventually come around.

For all that concerned her, Trish could always sleep. Regularly the last out of the house, she took to leaving earlier the last few days.

She hadn't realized Steve Sadler had been looking over her shoulder.

"That's quite a long list. Those things for the trip?" he asked.

"What? Oh yes. Do you believe all these last minute things I have to get? Preparing for a vacation is exhausting. There's so much to remember."

"I never get frantic when I travel. What's the worst that could happen? If you forget something, you buy it."

"I guess you're right," Trish said.

"Trish?"

"Yes?"

"What's bothering you?"

"Nothing. Everything. My desk's a mess. I've got all these forms to complete, and I promised you I would read the updated OSHA manual."

"It's more than that. We've been working together for,

what is it, five years? I know when your mind's somewhere else and it is definitely somewhere else."

Trish gazed blindly while he spoke. She looked up and saw his hazel eyes, his square chin, his upturned mouth. She felt his hand on her shoulder, and without warning, burst into tears, telling him everything.

"What I don't understand," she said, blowing her nose, "is how this could have occurred in the first place?" Steve leaned against the filing cabinet, a large wet stain laced with mascara blotched his shirt.

"Look, it happens. When I was a resident, nurses talked about wristbands falling off babies all the time. It's conceivable they put them back on the wrong babies."

"I can't accept that. Wouldn't you think there'd be a fool-proof method preventing this?"

"There is."

"What do you mean?"

"Footprints. Don't you remember that after every one of your children were born, a nurse took their footprints?"

"I never gave it much thought. I was more concerned about their Apgar scores. I couldn't wait for the nurse to tell me they were tens."

"Spoken like a true mother. But seriously, they take footprints because fingerprints are inaccurate on newborns. The problem is no one looks at them."

"But why not?" she asked.

"Who knows? Maybe it's inertia. Hospitals should verify that every baby's going home with the right family but they never bother. It seems kind of stupid, doesn't it?"

"Stupid is an understatement. This mess could've been avoided."

"I'm afraid so."

*   *   *

Gillian was engrossed in reading *Pride and Prejudice,* which was the first book she had to read before freshman orientation, and didn't hear the phone ring.

"It's for you," her mother called from the first floor. She reached for the phone.

"I've got incredible news!"

"You found your parents."

"Better than that, Gilly."

"Then what? Tell me."

"You have to guess."

"You're so mean to me."

"Guess."

"I give up! My mind's a blank."

"Here's a clue. What have we been dreaming about?"

"A trip to Paris. Going to the same college? What? I don't know."

"Buzzzzz. Wrong answer. For twenty points, University of Pennsylvania, can you answer the bonus question, and take the prize?"

"Phillip, you're torturing me. Did you buy me a present?"

"Wrong again! Buzzzzz. Contestant, we're now in the lightning round where all answers are worth double."

"Phillip! Enough, tell me!"

"Okay, okay, okay. Are you ready? This time next week, my folks and the Sturnweisses will be on their way to Portugal."

"Great! Will you and your brothers stay with Myrna?"

"No. Don't you get it? We're staying in our house."

"Alone?"

"Alone."

"My mother would never let me stay alone."

"Alone," he repeated.

"I can't believe they're trusting you like that."

"We'll have hours together and won't have to worry someone's going to interrupt us."

"I'll tell my mother I'll be out late," she whispered.

"And that you'll be starting early," he added.

They talked a while longer.

Phillip was too excited to fall asleep so he listened to the radio. Gillian, on the other hand, dropped off with an enormous grin on her face.

The next day, Brad was very busy. He and Tommy made room for the brass sockets the wily Sid Bergen was forced to make good on. The new catalogue was an immediate success; stock goods were ordered in larger quantities and many of the newly introduced items were tried. It wasn't always that way. From the get-go, Brad's father stymied his son's efforts to convert their small, retail electrical store into a wholesale, mail-order business. The senior Hunter refused to believe that customers would send money ahead of time, before they received their orders. "C.O.D.'s the way to go, Dad," Brad repeated mantra-like daily. It took his father's early death to allow Brad to follow his instincts.

The ceramic hobby industry exploded. Once a leisure-time activity for home-bound housewives, senior citizens, and arts and craft hobbyists, it grew, by economic necessity, into a way for many families to earn extra money. Brad was two steps ahead of the competition: he believed in well-stocked inventories that were often knock-offs from Taiwan or Korea making his profits larger. Each year, he saw to it that new items were introduced in the catalogue. CeramiElectric Mold Company's growth coincided with Newark's decline and the archaic three-floor walk-up was traded for a modern plant in the suburbs.

It was time to computerize. At his accountant's suggestion, Brad contacted a computer consultant on how to better manage the inventory.

John Davidson arrived by ten that morning. He was a systems analyst described by his accountant as an eccentric genius. He made every appliance in his house, from the washing machine to the television, from HeathKits. Though impressed, Brad wondered why a practical man would spend all his leisure time making things he could buy.

John had a sonorous voice, the kind that every choir master loved to find and keep. He spoke with extreme precision, wasting no words. His programs were just as precise, which meant they were fast, accurate, and free of bugs.

The pack of cigarettes he smoked during the two hour interview was reason enough not to hire him, but he was too knowledgeable to dismiss. One idea he had was to bar code the cartons of merchandise as they arrived. Electronic readers in the shipping area would regulate inventory and trigger supply needs. At the end of every month, the system would generate the customers' bills, evaluate the productivity of each worker, and record everyone's attendance. It even monitored hours worked, calculated fifteen minute breaks, and generated paychecks with the proper tax deductions.

"Excuse me, Mr. Hunter," Katie said over the intercom, "Phillip's waiting outside."

Brad turned to the computer consultant. He knew he needed this system. "John, I like what you have to say and my accountant says you're the best. You're hired. Send me a written proposal and let's get started."

"Thank you very much, Mr. Hunter. You'll have it on your desk by the beginning of next week." Brad knew he would.

Islands of dogwoods and birch trees in beds of white pebbles dotted the Lantellis' manicured lawn. Although water had been rationed for the last few months, their lawn was green. Brad and Phillip got out of the car as four boys emerged from the open garage, laughing and bouncing a basketball between them.

Brad and Phillip scrutinized each face, looking for a feature that would help identify the switched boy. Phillip wiped his sweaty palms on his pants. The ball seemed to move in slow motion, from one to the other, beckoning their eyes to focus on each of them. "It's me . . . no, it's me."

Walking down the driveway, Brad and Phillip centered on a lanky blond who weaved and bobbed and shot the ball with a confidence the other boys didn't display. He had an air of court sense, leadership. The boys continued to play as the strangers approached.

On the fourth note of the chime, a short, plump woman with red cheeks greeted them. She wore a flowery apron.

"Yes?"

"Are you Mrs. Lantelli?" Brad asked.

"Why, yes I am. May I help you?" Her pleasing smile was already in stark contrast to the wicked witch on Montana Drive. Practiced storytellers by now, Brad and Phillip stood at the open door, telling their story yet another time. Brad observed Mrs. Lantelli squinting, intent on catching every word.

". . . so could you tell us your blood type?" Brad asked.

"I'm not sure, Mr. Hunter," she said hesitantly.

"Not sure of what, Mrs. Lantelli? Your blood type?"

"No. That's not it, I know my blood type. You seem to be nice people but I'm not sure I should be talking to you. This story you described . . . it's so frightening. I mean I'm sympathetic to your problem and all that but it doesn't concern me or my boy." Her loosely clasped hands rested on her stomach.

Try as they might, she remained steadfast.

"Can you wait for my husband? He'll be home any minute.

Maybe he'll say it's okay." Joseph Lantelli soon pulled into the driveway in a cappuccino-colored Mercedes. The vanity tags read NINOS, which was the name of his restaurant in Morristown.

"Hey, Joey, throw your old man the ball." The gangling blond rifled it to him. The senior Lantelli's two-handed set shot hit the front of the rim and caromed to one of the waiting boys. Joseph Lantelli, Sr. gave the basket the finger and muttered an Italian curse and walked toward his wife and the two strangers.

"Joseph, this is Mr. Hunter and his son Phillip. They told me a story that might involve Joey and I told them they had to wait for you."

"What's the matter? Did Joey do something wrong?" He looked at Brad.

"No, Mr. Lantelli," Brad said, "it's nothing like that."

"You had me worried for a minute. Let's go inside. It's too hot to stand out here." Like the Capitol Building, marble covered every floor except the living room, which had a plush carpet that gave buoyancy to their steps. Phillip bounced to the sofa. The thick cushions were all but alive, swallowing him as he sat down. Brad took the opposite end of the sofa. They found themselves looking up at Mr. Lantelli, who was seated in a maroon paisley club chair opposite them.

All the furniture was Italian provincial, richly appointed and ornate in design. Sconces adorned the walls and hutches were laden with plates and servers. One shelf held mementos from the 1984 World's Fair and the Epcot Center. Sapphire crystal was carefully stowed on the top shelf and an imitation Tiffany lamp dangled over the black walnut dining room table.

Mrs. Lantelli excused herself and went into the kitchen to get lemonade for everyone. Brad repeated the story; this time, Phillip remained quiet, silenced by Mr. Lantelli's granite jaw. His laser-like stare penetrated Brad's practiced narration, making it difficult to maintain an even tempo. Though the house was air-conditioned, every few seconds, Brad wiped the sides of his face.

When he finished, the room was silent except for the ticking of the grandfather clock in the corner and the distant bouncing of a basketball. The Sicilian remained impassive; no part of his body moved except his cheek muscles, which beat rapidly. He cleared his throat and looked first to Phillip and then to his wife.

"Mr. Hunter," he began, "I feel for you and your son. I'm a father just like you, and every man wants to know who his children are . . ." He paused as if he were finished.

"I'm glad you agree, Mr. Lantelli." The man held up a short, stubby index finger that silenced him immediately.

"I'm not through. I sympathize with you but I'm not interested in any blood tests. Joey's my son." His index finger was raised in a gesture of solemn righteousness. "And he looks like his mamma," nodding once and throwing his head back.

"But, Mr. Lantelli, it's not only for Phillip and me, it's for. . . ." Again, the finger.

"Mr. Hunter. I see your problem. Believe me, I do. I'm not a stupid man. I've got a wonderful family but you have no business here." He stood and walked toward the door, dismissing them.

"Answer me this, Mr. Lantelli. What would you do if this happened to you? If the situation was reversed, how would you convince me your problem was my problem?"

"Sacred Mother, this is crazy." The senior Lantelli stopped walking and scratched his thick, wavy dark hair.

"Of course it's crazy! Would we be here if it weren't?"

"Okay, mister, you made your point. But how do I know

Phillip was born the same time my Joey was?" With the swiftness of a magician doing a card trick, Brad produced his son's birth certificate, Dr. Novick's letter, the hospital list and the lab report.

Mr. Lantelli took the evidence and sat down. Reaching for his pocket, he withdrew black-framed glasses from a leather case. Before putting them on, he wiped each lens with his handkerchief. He read them carefully, rereading each document twice. His eyes returned to the hospital list as he mouthed each name softly. Folding the papers neatly, he handed them back to Brad.

"Son?" He turned to Phillip for the first time, "What do you want?"

"I want to find out who my parents are. I don't want anything else, just to meet them." Phillip felt Mr. Lantelli's laser-stare probe his heart, penetrate his soul. Phillip squirmed, feeling naked beneath his gaze.

"So . . ." Joey's father said softly, slapping his knees with his large hands, "how can I help you?"

"We need to know your blood type and Mrs. Lantelli's, too."

"I don't know mine. What's yours, Ellie?"

"Mine is Type B. Let me get your Red Cross card in the kitchen, Joseph." They could hear a drawer slide open and papers being shuffled.

Brad looked at Phillip. "You realize," he said, "that if Mr. Lantelli is Type A, there could be a possibility." Phillip had already calculated that.

She walked into the room and turned rosy as everyone looked at her.

"It's Type B, too. Does that help you?"

Phillip and Brad's shoulders fell. "It means it can't be you."

"I'm glad Joseph said we could help you, Mr. Hunter, but I'm happy we're not the ones."

They turned to leave. "You've been very kind and understanding, thanks," Brad said.

The boys were still playing as Phillip got behind the driver's wheel. The tall blond boy drove to the basket, dribbled right, faked left, then pulled up and jumped. Whoosh! Strings only . . . no iron!

12

❧❧

"When are the Sturnweisses coming?" Brad asked Trish.

"At eight. They've been coming at eight for the last ten years." She snatched the bowl of peanuts just as he was taking some.

"You don't have to be so snippy," he said.

"Stating a fact is not being snippy, dear. Uh, aren't we being a little sensitive?" she asked.

"What do I have to be sensitive about?"

"Try guilt for carrying this DNA crap too far?" Trish put sourdough pretzels into what ordinarily served as a soup bowl. Next, she reached for a crystal ice bucket.

"Searching for a son is not crap!"

"No," she said and slammed the empty bucket on the counter, "then what would you call it? I am not missing any son. Why are you?"

"Oh, yes you are, you're just afraid to admit it." He opened the refrigerator door. Seeing nothing he wanted, he shut it.

"Don't you want to know what happened at the Lantellis' today?"

"Nope. Not interested."

Brad grabbed her by the shoulders and spun her around,

catching an ice cube as it flew off the top.

"How could you not. . . ."

The doorbell rang. Brad let them in. Susan led Rick into the kitchen, her pace coming to a halt. She lifted her nose and twitched her nostrils.

"Whew! I smell an argument. Rick and I left our gas masks back at the bunker. We'll return when the all-clear sirens have been sounded."

"Stop right there, you two. I'm glad you came, Sue. Brad and I have something to tell you and now's as good a time as any."

"Hey, I hope you guys aren't . . . ," Rick made the motion of slicing his open palm in half with his right hand, ". . . splitting."

"No," Brad said, "nothing like that. Let's go inside."

Instead of dealing the cards, Brad described everything from Frank Bellman's first suspicion that Phillip wasn't theirs to the encounter with the Lantellis that day.

"So who do you see next?" Sue asked.

"There's not much choice. We found seven names. We eliminated the first and the last assuming no one would confuse a newborn with a baby three days older or younger than it. That left five names. We've visited two families without any luck," omitting the fact that Mrs. Schwartz wasn't cooperative, "so we're down to three. Today, we located the family of Winfield Arlen Jones, III."

"Where do they live?" Rick asked.

"Mt. Laurel, except no one answers their phone."

"Maybe they're on vacation," Susan said.

"Sounds rich to me. They don't have homes in Mt. Laurel, they have mansions. At least Phillip wouldn't have to keep up with the Joneses; he'll be one, and a rich one at that."

"Not funny, Rick," Brad said.

"Ouch, what'd you kick me for?" Rick turned to Sue. She

put her index finger under her chin and smiled broadly, all lips and no teeth. The corners of her mouth turned up, forming dimples in her plump cheeks.

"Why are you such an asshole sometimes, Rick?"

"Because then you can appreciate me when I'm not."

"Cool it, guys. I'm trying to find my son and you're making jokes."

"*I'm* trying to find my son," Trish said in a high, squeaky voice. "I'm fed up with this righteous bullshit about helping Phillip and looking for a missing son."

"Whoa, Trish, you may not like this, but I agree with Brad. He's right to help Phillip," Sue said.

"Not you, too! I thought you were my friend."

"I am your friend and that's why I'm telling you you're making a mountain out of a mole hill. Phillip needs your help, he's curious about his background. That's normal," Sue said.

"And you?" Trish looked at Rick.

"I'm not sure. As a parent. . . ."

"You mean as a father." Trish corrected him.

"Okay, as a father, I would like to know who my children are."

"That's not the issue, Rick. The question is whether you'd search for this biological son after raising a boy you thought was your own. After all, isn't Phillip our son? Why look for this other child unless. . . ."

"Unless what?" Brad asked. Trish waved her hand at the walls.

"Look at those pictures, Brad. Vacations, holidays . . . and it's more than that. What do you call changing diapers, staying up when your child's burning with a fever, or being there when he takes his first step? *That's* what it means to be a parent. You can't throw those experiences away. Phillip is our son and I'm his mother."

111

Brad struggled to swallow. Trish was at the edge of her chair; she looked from one to the other. Her lips quivered as one drop after another rolled down her cheeks. She leaped from the table, the chair legs squeaking on the polished wooden floor, and without another word, ran out of the room.

While Trish was fleeing, Phillip was intertwined with Gillian. Mrs. Davis's frequent interruptions had forced them to abandon Gillian's basement for the insured privacy of his Jeep. No longer worried about her mother, their partially clad bodies tensed with every passing headlight reflecting off the fogged windows.

"Ouch," she said, "you bit me."

"Sorry. I got carried away," Phillip said through his teeth, still sucking her nipple. He cupped the other breast and pushed her blouse further around her neck.

"That's sooooo romantic," she said and pushed it away to breathe. He lifted his head, glimpsed her partially blocked face, smiled, and dove back for more. She yanked his hair.

"Did I hurt you again?"

"No, but this isn't fun."

"What do you mean? It's great."

"For you. What do you expect me to do while you're sucking my tits?"

"I thought you enjoyed this."

"It's not very personal, Phillip. Try being tender. Kiss me."

"I love you, Gilly."

"And I love you, silly." She wrapped her arms around him and kissed him, thrusting her tongue deep inside his mouth. She nibbled on his ear and licked it, driving him wild.

"Hey, easy. You're twisting them too hard."

"Sorry. It's just that you get me so excited, I lose control. I'm ready to explode. I can't wait until we. . . ."

112

"Neither can I."

"Don't you want to . . . to touch me? It's so big and it's beginning to hurt."

She smiled. "Does it hurt bad?"

"Uh huh."

"And you want me to relieve you?"

"Uh huh."

"Okay, I will."

"You will?"

"Yup, right now." Phillip started pulling down his zipper. He heard the door click. "Hey, where're you going?"

"H-O-M-E. That's how I spell relief."

"Gillian. How can you make fun of me when I'm in pain. My balls are killing me. If you don't help me, I'm afraid that . . . ."

"Cut the crap. All guys say the same thing: *If you don't relieve me, I'll get blue balls.* Go home and jerk off in the shower."

"Gilly, please?"

"Chill out, Phillip. I want to do it just as much as you—but we agreed to wait until your parents are away."

"I know, but I really am in pain."

"I'm sure you are, but you'll have to wait a little longer."

13

🌱🌱

Myrna was drinking her morning coffee when Frank walked into the kitchen wearing white tennis shorts and an Adidas navy shirt. Horizontal red stripes ran across it, accentuating his flabby mid-section.

"Don't we have to get to the court?"

"I just got off the phone with Trish and she told me your hair experiment has gotten out of control. There was quite a scene at their bridge game last night."

"I swear to God, I never thought it would get this far. I figured after I told Brad and Trish, they would forget about it. Honest."

"But they didn't, did they?"

He pulled out a kitchen chair, its legs dragging on the kitchen tile. Myrna handed him a cup of coffee and watched him take it to his lips.

"Why'd you do it, Frank?" He stared into the black liquid, watching an air bubble float on the surface. "What did you think it'd accomplish?"

"I thought I was doing the right thing, hon. Once I found out that Phillip probably wasn't theirs, I had to bring it to their attention. That's all."

"Frank, these are real people. They're not specimens in

one of your laboratory experiments. Trish and Brad have put their lives into raising those boys. I know I would never have told them."

He swiveled to face Myrna. "I'm a scientist. I solve problems. When Phillip asked for help, I gave it to him. I really wasn't thinking; I saw a puzzle and tried to solve it. It was nothing more than that, I promise you. It was a goddamned puzzle," he said, burying his face in his hands.

"Did you have to be so truthful, Frank?"

"You expect me to lie when something's so obviously wrong?"

"You could've looked the other way. How hard would it have been?"

"I did that once and look what happened." Frank recalled the day he was summoned to the Dean's office.

"I'm not going to mince words with you, Bellman. We're in hot soup. The Office of Scientific Integrity is sending their goon squad to review all research using federal grant money at the medical school. The president of the university is furious. How could you do it, Frank?"

"Do what, Dean?"

"Falsify the data on your last paper."

"Have you gone mad? I've never falsified anything in my life. I don't know what you're talking about."

"I wish that was the case. Let me start from the beginning. Recently, you submitted a paper on the prevalence of the HIV virus in the school-age children of Cook County."

"I was the senior author. Bernstein, Lewiston, and Sanchez were the chief investigators."

"Well, it seems Sanchez has sued the university, the New England Journal of Medicine, you, me, and Lewiston, along with blabbing to the government."

"What for? Is this some kind of joke?"

"I'm afraid not. You see, Sanchez never wanted that arti-

cle published. She said the data were bogus and publishing it would hurt her career."

"She never said anything to me. I was very careful with the data."

"Sanchez recognized the pattern of numbers. Lewiston, it turns out, never got around to every school. Trying to meet the deadline, he used blood collected from another study."

"But the only samples in the lab were from the county jail study."

"Precisely. Knowing this, Sanchez confronted Lewiston. He ridiculed her, of course, leaving Sanchez no alternative. What are you going to do about it? You're the senior author."

"Why me? I've been so busy raising my boy since my wife died. How can you expect me to check every piece of work coming out of my lab?"

"Sorry about your wife. But that doesn't excuse you from. . . ."

"Frank, you're not listening to me. You, of all people, should value the consequences of taking the blame for something beyond your control. You should've stopped it, Frank. It's Chicago all over again."

"But that's lying."

"There are times when you have to. Sometimes the truth serves no purpose. Look, you did what you thought was right. I guess that's one of the reasons I love you."

"What do you think will happen?" he asked.

"Phillip only wants to meet his biological parents. Right? So when he finds them, his curiosity will be satisfied and that'll be the end of it. I'm sure of it."

"I hope you're right, Myrna."

"So do I," she said.

Sunday morning, Phillip limped into the kitchen. "What did you say, Dad?" Phillip and Gillian had been to the Jersey

Shore Saturday, and he had fallen asleep for several hours. The pain from the sunburn was intense.

"I was talking to myself. Whoever invented oat bran muffins should have their bodies coated with honey and made to stand next to a beehive. Ever eat one?" He brandished one in the air, holding it like a shot put.

"But they're good for you."

"Yeah? Who says?" Brad took another bite and grimaced. "That's it. I've had enough! Are there any doughnuts left, or did the human garbage disposal polish them all off?"

"I think Todd left a couple."

"Great!"

Finding two chocolate-covered doughnuts, they chatted about baseball scores and when they thought Michael Jordan would leave basketball and become a professional golfer. Then, Brad recited his annual "God-forbid-but-I-want-you-to-know-where-everything-is" speech.

"Dad, we've been through this a hundred times. First, I go to the vault and take everything out; then I call Murray Braverman about your insurance policies. I sell the business to Bluebird Mold Company and buy tax-exempt CDs."

"I know you hate talking about it but someone has to know what to do just in case. . . ."

"Dad, nothing's going to happen."

"I hope not. Are you sure you have it straight?"

"Daaaaaad."

"Just checking, just checking." Brad held his hands up. "What are we going to do about your BPs?" They had come to call his phantom biological parents, *BPs*. It was simpler, and no one had to know what they were talking about.

"Except for Winfield Jones, the easy stuff is over. Who knows? We could end up at the Schwartzes' again," Phillip said. "If we do, we'd better bring a lion tamer."

"Cute. Let's hope it doesn't come to that. You know we're

117

leaving Wednesday. Can you wait until we get back from Portugal?"

"No sweat. I'm bummed out from all of this. It's taken eighteen years for this to come out—eight more days won't matter." Phillip winced as he stood up.

"Hey, where're you going?" Brad asked. Phillip hobbled across the kitchen floor.

"Gillian's waiting for me. We volunteered to be in a walk-a-thon for muscular dystrophy. You remember the church is raising money for Jerry's kids on the Labor Day Telethon."

"You're not going to get very far. You can barely stand."

"Don't count me out, Dad. I'll go the distance."

"I'm sure you will, Phillip."

14

❦❦

Phillip stared out the dark tinted windows of Parker Pharmaceuticals, reliving his day at the beach with Gillian. He smiled recalling how he maneuvered his hammer into her palm as she slept on the blanket, and how she jumped up when she realized what she was holding.

"How's it going?" Frank asked. Phillip grabbed his chest, startled by the unexpected interruption. Frank held up his hands. "Take it easy. I didn't mean to scare you. A bomb could have gone off and you wouldn't have heard it."

"I was . . . thinking about something."

"That was obvious."

"About my BPs."

"Your what?"

"My biological parents, that's what my dad and I call them. We've got the address of one more name and then we're stuck."

"Maybe they'll be the ones."

"I hope so. I'm getting tired of this," Phillip said.

"Can I help you with the other names?"

"We've exhausted everything we could think of short of hiring a detective."

"Where did the fathers work?" Frank asked.

"In Mr. Ruderman's case, the business no longer exists, and Mr. Manning didn't list any place of employment."

"What did Ruderman do?"

"He was a shoe salesman."

"Hold on, that's a lead. Call up the hospital administrator and. . . ."

Phillip dashed to the phone.

"Mr. Johnson, there's a call for you on line four."

"Who is it, Yolanda?"

"It's that Hunter boy. You know, the one who was switched," she said, making a snapping noise into the receiver.

"Thanks, Yolanda, and spit out your gum, please."

"Phillip? Ezekial Johnson here. How you doing?"

"Pretty well, sir. We've struck out so far. But I need a favor."

"And what might that be, boy?"

"We have no leads on the Rudermans or the Mannings. Mr. Ruderman worked in a shoe store but it was destroyed in the riots."

"A lot of things were destroyed in '68."

"I was wondering if Ms. Bathgate could check if we overlooked something that might help, like a next of kin or anything that might be a clue. There must be something we missed."

A prolonged silence followed. Here comes the bad news, Phillip thought, dreading the administrator's answer.

"This is highly irregular, Phillip. I can't give out that kind of information without a release from the Rudermans and the Mannings."

"That's okay with me, Mr. Johnson. If you find them, you can ask them!"

"I see your point, but it still doesn't persuade me to help you. Let me sleep on it. I'll call you tomorrow."

True to his word, Ezekial Johnson called the following day.

"Research lab," Frank said.

"Phillip Hunter, please. It's Ezekial Johnson."

"Hold on, Mr. Johnson, he's expecting your call." Frank placed the receiver on his desk and poked his head into the hall. Phillip was rounding the corner, pulling two heavy Purina Chow bags in a small red wagon. "Phillip, your Mr. Johnson's on the phone." Hearing the name, Phillip dropped the black metal handle and raced to the office.

"It's Phillip, Mr. Johnson," he said huffing.

"Good morning, Phillip." The hospital administrator waited for Phillip's response.

"Oh, good morning," Phillip said, finding his manners.

"Mr. Ruderman worked in a shoe store on Bergen Street which closed, as you know, but I found something that might help us," Ezekial Johnson said. The "us" did not escape Phillip. "It seems part of their bill was paid by the Retail Sales Union. Selling shoes gets into your blood, same as circus-life gets into some people. I bet our man's still in the union. Give them a call, the office is in East Orange."

"That's great! And what about the Mannings?" Phillip heard paper shuffling through the ear piece. "Are you there, Mr. Johnson?"

"Hold your horses, boy. I'm looking through the chart right now. No . . . no . . . that's no help," he said out loud. Phillip waited and read the poster on the far wall for the first time: *YOUR ONLY LIMITATION IN LIFE IS YOUR OWN IMAGINATION.* "Here's something. An SMA 12. Phillip, I'll call you right back."

He picked it up on the first ring.

"Phillip? Is that you?"

"It's me. What's going on?"

"When I found the SMA 12, it gave me the idea that. . . ."

"What's an SMA 12?"

"Oh, that's a routine blood test. Seems I missed it before. But when I was talking with you, the bilirubin was high. Lots of babies are born with high bilirubin counts, but the Manning baby's was too high. So I had Ms. Bathgate check, and sure enough, a David Manning was admitted two weeks later."

"The same David Manning?"

"Definitely. He was three weeks old, born on March 22, 1975 to Sally and Thomas. Same one. And. . . ."

"Yes?"

". . . they took his blood type."

"What was it?" Phillip squeezed his lips.

"A."

"Are you sure?"

"Phillip, I know an A when I see one!"

"That eliminates David Manning."

"Why so certain?"

"Because my mother's O and my father's B. They couldn't have a Type A baby."

"Too bad, Phillip."

"No, this is great. The Mannings are off the list and you gave me an important lead. I'm getting closer."

"Phillip? Keep me informed."

"I will, Mr. Johnson. Later."

Frank stood nearby.

"Any luck?"

"The Manning baby can be ruled out, he was admitted three weeks later and his blood type was A. And a union paid part of the Rudermans' bill."

"So who's left?"

Phillip held up two fingers. "It's either the Rudermans or the Joneses. I'll go to the Joneses when my parents return. God, I hope they're the ones."

Last minute directives were given to everyone: Brad gave them to Tommy while Trish gave them to the nurse who covered for her at Steve Sadler's office. Instructions were stated and restated to Phillip, Todd, and Ron, making certain they would call Myrna if they needed anything.

The charter plane left Kennedy Airport two hours late. The summer's prolonged heat spell cut the utility's power outage by five percent, leaving the departure lounge a sweltering hot box. The windows couldn't be opened and the stifling air suffocated. Clothes clung to drenched bodies.

"It was unbearable in there. I hope the plane is better," Trish said, handing her boarding pass to the flight attendant who managed to look like she just left a refrigerated room.

"I'm afraid not. Only regularly scheduled planes get power to run the air-conditioning while boarding. They're connected to the gates. Charter planes are not hooked up to the electricity. I'm sorry for the inconvenience."

Trish shot an angry look to Brad.

"Hey, it's not my fault. You made the arrangements."

"I know. It's killing me. I can't even blame you."

They sat down with Rick and Susan across the aisle, and leafed through magazines while the remaining passengers filed onto the overheated plane. Many carried large packages and infants or both. The process was painfully slow.

"We better take off soon. The odor's killing me," Sue said, pinching her nostrils together.

Brad surveyed the number of empty seats. "It won't be much longer," he said. Moments later, the last passenger was seated and the engines came to life. The plane vibrated, and, with a shudder, taxied onto the runway. Once airborne, the cabin became cooler and air freshener was pumped through the ventilation system, reviving them. Finally comfortable, they settled in for an uneventful flight.

Arriving in Lisbon around 7:45 A.M., they bypassed customs and caught the flight to the southern city of Faro with five minutes to spare. The small jet carried the forty-five passengers over mountains carpeted with olive groves. Small villages sprinkled the hillsides, connected to the main thoroughfare by roads Roman warriors had once marched on. Brad pictured a scene below: rainbow-clad Gypsies carrying their life's possessions in wooden wagons while passing shepherds who guided flocks around dangerous mountain turns.

"Do you think the pilot knows what he's doing?" Rick whispered to Brad.

"I think so."

"I get real nervous when the pilot speaks a foreign language and the plane's instruction manual is in English," Rick said with a nervous laugh.

Just then, the plane veered to the left and the mountains dissolved into flat, dry terrain. Barely missing a church steeple, they landed on a small airstrip a few kilometers from the Spanish border.

Soldiers in khaki uniforms, with black patent leather holsters strapped to their sides, passed them through immigration. While Rick and Brad loaded their luggage onto the roof of their rented car, Trish and Sue exchanged U.S. dollars for Portuguese escudos. With the ocean to their left and sleepy villages built on scraggly hills on the right, they drove to Abufeira. Speeding vehicles kicked up dust clouds from the stretches of unfinished roads. And every so often, they were forced to stop to let a donkey or an ox-cart cross the highway.

"Is that the Mediterranean?" Susan asked.

"No, that's the Atlantic," Trish answered. "The Mediterranean begins at Gibraltar. We're on the ocean side of Europe." Like vacations in the past, roles were defined: Brad drove and held their collective monies while Trish navigated. Rick scouted the best places to eat and studied which wines to drink, and Sue taught them local customs and idiomatic expressions, none of which they could ever say correctly.

About the same time Trish, Brad, Sue and Rick found Casa de la Mar, a white stuccoed building with a red-orange tiled roof, Phillip was in the middle of taking inventory of glass pipettes. His thoughts wandered to the call he needed to make. He took a step forward and stopped. The open door beckoned. He licked his lips, then shook his head. "I can't do it," he said. Returning to the stock case, his reflection in the tinted window caused him to pivot. "To the rear— march!" Phillip stepped inside his uncle's empty office.

"Retail Sales Union, McGarret speaking."

"Mr. McGarret? I'm trying to locate one of your members. Can you help me?" he asked in a practical tone.

"Who are you and why do you want to know?" the gruff voice shot back. With fingers crossed, Phillip calmly explained he was looking for a friend from camp, that he knew they moved but didn't know where. McGarret asked a few more questions and then barked, "Wait a minute." Phillip would have waited an eternity for the right answer.

"Here it is," he said. "Morris Ruderman . . . that's him, ain't it?"

"Yessir!"

"Okay, then. Sixteen-twenty-one Franklin Avenue, Somerset, New Jersey. Got it?" McGarret said.

"Got it!"

Now he had the address of the last name. It was narrowed down to the Joneses and the Rudermans. But there was little time to reflect on this small victory—he had much to do before Gillian came over that night.

15

🌱🌱

Phillip squinched to avoid getting soap in his eyes. He scrubbed harder than he normally did, feeling layers of skin peel away beneath the square wash cloth. Depeche Mode, M.C. Hammer, Madonna, and others blared on MTV while the bar of Irish Spring glided on his private equipment. The creamy soap lubricated the delicate skin and his deliberate up and down movements made it come alive. Pleasure filled his body as his hand moved faster and faster. Phillip leaned against the shower wall enjoying the tingling feeling, but stopped short of the point of no return. The last thing he wanted to do was come in the shower and ruin the evening he had planned for so long.

Phillip shaved while avoiding any tugs that might nick his face, though it was hard to cut himself with an electric shaver. Splashing on some Aqua Velva, he combed his hair and got dressed. He put on a blue-striped oxford shirt and pleated khaki pants with inch-and-a-half cuffs. A roped belt and brown docksiders without socks completed his ensemble.

Whistling as he went down the stairs, he ducked into the den for one last check. He lowered the lights and readied Ottmar Liebert's latest compact disc.

He picked up Gillian. She wore a red camisole and a white skirt.

"Like some music?"

"Sure," Gillian said. The flamenco guitar boosted their excitement. "You've planned this down to the last detail, haven't you?"

"Want a drink?" Phillip asked.

"Diet Coke, please. By the way, where're your brothers?"

"Oh, lucky for us, they went to a ball game. The guys wanted to see Clemens pitch." The bribe had cost him two tickets to the Yankee/Boston game plus $50 spending money. Phillip scampered to and from the kitchen, stumbling over the area rug, nearly spilling the soda on her.

More like a clod than a graceful date, Phillip plopped onto the couch next to her. He was uncomfortable. He tapped his shoe on the floor and watched her drink. She smiled. Phillip's shirt rubbed against his neck, and the couch fabric felt like flax through his pants. The sensuous music played on; they stared at each other, both unsure. Gillian took matters into her own hands and kissed him. Phillip moved closer, their legs touched. His hands explored her bare shoulders. A soft moan escaped from deep within her.

"Can we get more comfortable?" he asked. By now, he was lying on top of her.

"What did you have in mind?"

"Let's go upstairs." He extended a hand to help her, which she did not take.

"Aren't you taking me for granted?"

"Gilly, stop kidding. We couldn't wait for my parents to go to Portugal. Why did you think I got Ron and Todd the baseball tickets?"

"Cool it. I didn't want to make it too easy." She swung her legs onto the floor. "Let's go upstairs, but you have to promise we'll be good." He agreed.

They made their way to his room. He reached for the wall switch.

"Could you keep the lights off, please?"

She looked at the window. Phillip drew the blinds, eliminating the light from the halogen street lamp. The only light in the room came from the glowing dials of his clock radio. They waited for their eyes to become accustomed to the cave-like shadows.

Phillip found Gillian on the bed, her bra refastened. He kicked his docksiders off and lay next to her. The stillness of the room was punctuated by her short, shallow breaths. He watched her chest go up and down until they were breathing in cadence. They kissed. His lips caressed her eyelids, the edge of her ear and the nape of her neck. She groaned. His leg climbed on top of hers, guided by a will of its own. She didn't protest or resist as in the past.

After a few moments, Gillian squirmed from under him and removed her blouse. Phillip watched the ease with which Gillian undressed. Covering her chest, she stepped into his arms, and his lips drifted over her shoulder, finding the softness of her breasts. Mindful of past warnings, Phillip gently mouthed her nipples, feeling them spring alive to the flick of his tongue. Their hips drew together, their bodies fused into one.

He found the buttons to her cloth skirt and began undoing them one by one, waiting for the reprimand which didn't come. So far, so good. Still no objection when the unmistakable noise of his zipper was heard. Their breathing became heavier. Gillian waited. The next move was his. A message was transmitted to all parts of his taut body: *this was no training mission.* He tugged and she arched her back, wiggling out of the skirt. He stared into her eyes, afraid to look at her naked body. Lips together, he jackknifed each leg out of his pants.

The tempo picked up as their bodies pressed together. Her legs parted. He tried to penetrate her damp panties through his boxer shorts.

"Stop! I don't think this is a good idea, Phillip."

"My God, Gilly, we planned on it! It'll be good, I promise."

"Not now, okay?"

"What do you mean, 'not now'? We couldn't be more ready, you're wet as can be and I'm a missile ready to explode."

She ignored his plea and drew his face to hers. Phillip wondered how to convince her when he felt her fingertips grope against his skin. At first, he didn't realize what she was doing. Then he felt the waistband roll over on itself and slide down his leg.

"Now yours," he said.

"No. This is far enough. Besides, you don't have protection."

"Yes, I do. My father gave me two dozen rubbers last summer in case I needed them. He tried to tell me about the biological urges but I told him he was five years too late."

"How many do you have left?"

"All but one."

"You told me you never did it before!"

"It's true; I haven't! I used one for practice." They stopped talking and kissed some more. On one of his accidental/deliberate passes over her thigh, he nudged her panties aside. This time, she didn't stop him. Clumsily, he felt her moist hairs. He touched different spots until one bit of prominent flesh caused her to gasp. Phillip felt the delicate skin swell.

"Softer," she said.

Her legs thrashed on the bed as he penetrated her with his fingers.

"Please, Phillip. Hurry. Hurry." As he rolled off her, Gillian removed her panties. Phillip reached into the night table drawer and got the partially opened condom. Despite his earlier preparation, he fumbled with the foil wrapper. The cold wet rubber wouldn't roll down. He tried again, worried his erection would fail him.

"Shit! It's defective!"

"No it's not." Gillian took it from him and flipped it over. It had been upside down.

Guiding him, Gillian felt him penetrate. She bit her lip, her eyes watered.

"Please don't hurt me," she whispered. Her body stiffened and she remained quiet. He pushed harder when he felt resistance. His penis hurt. He pushed again. "Phillip, don't push. Go in and out . . . slowly." He followed her instructions afraid the condom would roll on itself or, worse yet, fall off. The mattress sang in a cushioned rhythm to his thrusts. Then, like the sun emerging from behind a cloud, her pain disappeared. Gillian groaned.

Phillip pumped in and out. He closed his eyes. In and out. Then, like a painful hiccup, he felt a squirt, a smaller one, then he was finished. He held himself above her, motionless, afraid to move. His legs no longer felt connected to him. He was numb. Start to finish, it took thirty, maybe thirty-five seconds!

Phillip groped for the thickened lip of latex, like his gym teacher said to do in health class. It slid off.

"Are you okay?" he asked. She nodded, her hands crossed over her breasts. "Did it hurt?"

"A little," she answered.

"I tried to be gentle."

"I know you did. It's supposed to hurt the first time." The room was dark. Their breathing became shallow again, like they were afraid to disturb the air. "I didn't know it would be like this," she said softly.

"Was it . . . did it feel good?"

"One part did. I guess it gets better each time. I'm glad I did it with you. I couldn't have done it with anyone else."

"Me, too." He wanted to look at Gillian but felt self-conscious, like he was a voyeur. So he stared at the ceiling.

"Did you like it?" she asked.

"It kind of hurt. I thought it would've felt better. I guess I didn't know what to expect." He turned and she rolled into his arms. They cuddled for many minutes.

"Gilly? I was scared," he confessed.

"So was I," she said into his chest.

"Gilly?"

"Yes, Phillip?"

"I love you."

"I love you, too."

The piercing rays of the Portuguese sun baked their skin, in spite of layers of number fifteen sun block. Trish took her bathing suit off in front of Brad's admiring eyes. Her skin glowed except for the small areas covered by the skimpy material. Her breasts, in stark contrast, were white; the sight of her rose-red nipples aroused him. Brad walked over to her as she combed the knots out of her hair. She lurched away.

"I thought you wanted to take a nap?" she asked.

"I did 'til I saw how beautiful you look. I can't help it if you turn me on after all these years." He tried to kiss her.

"Why don't we take a nap. You know I don't like to make love during the day. Later, we'll see what happens. Deal?"

"What kind of deal is that? We're on vacation!"

"So's this." She pointed to her crotch.

"I guess you're not in the mood."

"You could say that."

They got into bed and in no time, Brad was fast asleep.

Trish tossed and turned, unable to find a comfortable position. The sheets felt cold next to her burnt skin. With eyes failing to close, she reviewed the events of the past three weeks. Fragments of conversations swirled in her brain, talks she had with Sue, Brad, and Steve Sadler. She turned to Brad, wishing he would hold her, wishing he would make everything better.

16

🌿🌿

The search for Winfield Arlen Jones III took Phillip south, past eyesores of urban progress or industrial blight, depending on one's point of view. Though referred to as the "garden state," New Jersey is better known for the foul-odored swamps of the Meadowlands, mountain-high garbage dumps, and hundreds of white containers filled with crude oil that line the Turnpike like fields of poisonous metallic mushrooms. Travellers between New York and Philadelphia must roll up their car windows and insulate themselves from the putrid smoke from burning gas pipes and the unrelenting noise of Newark International Airport. Yet with every passing exit, the foul air melts further away. Unused warehouses give way to glitzy industrial parks built in concert with the environment, surrounded by fields of corn and grazing cows. Leaving the toll-road, the land changes once more to a panorama of rolling hills and luscious meadows filled with wild flowers and orchards of fruit trees. Horses can be seen prancing playfully on lands inherited by the families of the once-great barons, their mansions perched on hilltops overlooking their sprawling estates.

Phillip asked a gas attendant for directions, but couldn't be blamed for missing the cutoff; the tiny bridge was not a bridge at all, but a jumble of wooden planks barely stretching over a meandering creek. He felt the boards sink and shift under the Jeep's weight. Halfway across, he gunned the motor, figuring his momentum would get him to the other side even if the bridge collapsed.

"If Evel Knievel can do it, so can I," he said gripping the steering wheel, braced for anything.

Safely across, he continued until he saw a white stone marker bearing a bronze plaque: CHATEAU LIBERTÉ/The Joneses. Phillip ignored the "No Trespassing" sign and went ahead. In the distance loomed an enormous house, a modern-day Tara that overlooked the picturesque valley. As he approached the Chateau, the dirt road became covered with white pebbles that matched the color of the house. Phillip parked under a columned portico and opened the door as a uniformed butler hurried to assist him. He brought to mind Sir John Gielgud, and he bowed deeply from the waist.

"May I be of service, young man?"

"Uh . . . is this the Jones residence or did I end up at a country club?"

"This is the Jones residence. Are you expected?"

"Not exactly. My name is Phillip Hunter and I need to speak with Mr. Jones. It's very important. Is he home?"

"Mr. Jones is preparing for his morning ride. I'll see if he will receive you, Master Hunter," the butler said bowing again.

"Thank you." Phillip returned the bow. The angular footman with a lean face and all-knowing eyes, screamed to be called "Jeeves." Phillip followed him and wondered what his Christian name might be. He did not miss the champagne-colored Bentley next to the red Ferrari Testarossa alongside the mansion. If his BPs were the Joneses, this wasn't going to be so bad!

"Wait here." Phillip stood on the veranda, which was as

long as a bowling alley. He looked through a window; antiques were everywhere. Tiffany lamps held by linked chains dangled above over-sized leather chairs and couches, the kind one expected to find in the Harvard Club. Stuffed animal heads jutted from the walls; there was a moose and a brown bear, along with a red fox and smaller animals he didn't recognize. On the far wall was an enormous marlin. A gun rack neatly stacked with hunting rifles occupied the corner.

Phillip took inventory through the window when he heard footsteps behind him.

"Do I know you?" the tall man asked in a clipped voice, a riding crop in one hand.

"Are you Mr. Jones?"

"Yes. What can I do for you?" Phillip followed his lead and backed into the wicker chair behind him; groping for the arm rest, he sat down.

"My name is Phillip Hunter, Mr. Jones. I was born the same day your son was . . . at the Beth. March 21."

"That's right, March 21. That makes you and Junior eighteen."

Phillip studied Winfield Jones. His hair was shorter than Phillip's but just as wavy. His skin was smooth. He didn't have to shave very often but managed to grow a small, wispy moustache above his upper lip. His eyes were full of determination, and though he reclined, his body looked like a coiled spring, ready to leap.

"There were others in the nursery besides me and your son. I've found most of them already."

"Who are you looking for, Phillip?" He hit his outstretched palm with his riding crop.

"My parents."

"Who do you live with now?"

"My parents."

He raised his eyebrows. Unlike Brad, Phillip could see no wrinkles on Winfield Jones's face.

"It's complicated. . . ."

So Phillip Hunter explained what had happened to him over the last three weeks, beginning with his interest in genetically bred laboratory animals and ending with Ezekial Johnson eliminating the Manning boy.

". . . and that's about it."

"I'm sorry for you, Phillip. You've been through so much. It must be getting you down."

"Kind of. Anyway, I need to know your blood type . . . and your wife's, too."

"If it will do you any good, mine is Type B and Mrs. Jones has O. As soon as you said yours was AB, I knew we couldn't be the ones."

"Too bad," Phillip said looking around. "This is a nice place."

"Thank you, Phillip. Come back and visit if you want. If nothing else, my son and you have something in common. I'm sure he'd like to meet you."

"Thank you, Mr. Jones. I'd like to meet him, too. Maybe when this is settled, I'll come back. Thanks again."

Phillip ambled to his Jeep. He started the engine and looked at the pillared house one last time . . . and sighed.

Once on the main road, he pulled into the gas station he had stopped in earlier for directions and called Gillian.

"Ben and Jerry's Ice Cream Parlor."

"Gilly, it's me. You won't believe what happened."

"It's them, isn't it? I knew it would be. Is Mr. Jones nice?"

"The nicest. You should see their mansion. But it's not him. I knew it the minute we met."

"How can you be so sure?"

137

"Because as white as my skin is, that's how black Winfield Arlen Jones's is."

Unseen currents from the North Sea kept all but the heartiest swimmers out of the frigid Algarve waters. Brad and Trish walked along the beach, skirting the cold surf with their bare feet. Brad watched her plod through the sand, her chin hung low. She never looked at him. Soon, large rock formations blocked their way; they could go no further. Brad tugged at her arm to reverse directions.

"Do you love me?" she asked.

"You know I do. How can you ask?"

"Because this thing with Phillip makes me doubt it."

"Shit, can't you get it through your sun-fried brain that I care about you and the family? That's why I'm doing this. What other motivation could I have? You know, Trish, this works two ways. How come you don't support what I'm doing? I'm tired of you challenging me, making me out to be the bad guy."

"Maybe it's that gender thing, the way men and women speak different languages. I say one thing, you hear something else. You feel you're helping the family, I think it's threatening. You say you love me, I know you can't."

"Love, love, love, that's all you talk about lately. Have I done anything to make you insecure? Doubt my feelings for you?"

"That's the point, this has *everything* to do about respecting my wishes. Since you haven't respected them, you can't possibly love me. The two go together. Do you get it now? or do I have to paint you a picture? This . . . this nightmare has taught me that I took your love for granted. I guess I assumed too much."

"Let's discuss this when you're more rational."

"Me? Irrational? I was the one willing to forget the whole

thing and not tell Phillip. I was the rational one!"

Trish stomped toward the rocks ahead, sending sprays of salt water in the air.

"Where do you think you're going?"

The distance between them quickly increased. Brad felt helpless. He called after her but his words were drowned by the thunderous waves. He started to run but stopped; she needed time to sort things out. She would come to her senses, he knew she would. And besides, he didn't want to face her; these confrontations reminded him of when he tried to argue with his parents and always lost.

The beach gave way to a sudden rise. A path led to the top of the limestone cliff where Trish stood upon a plateau covered with stinging coarse grass. Without something to grab onto, she peered over the edge. The steep drop ended in swirling eddies that crashed into the rocks that had been covered a billion years earlier when the world's water table was higher. Now receded, the pounding waves sent its icy spray four stories high into her face.

Needing to free herself of her anger at Brad, Trish loped across the elevation, dancing and whirling when she nearly tumbled into a large hole. She crawled to the edge. Sunlight beamed through the opening onto a small beach below. Feeling adventuresome, Trish placed her foot over the perimeter and found a foothold, carefully making her way to the bottom. It was a cave with two exits or entrances depending on how you saw things; one from the top and the other from the sea. The surf blocked the seaward entrance, and, at this time of day with an incoming tide, there was only one way in or out. Trish had discovered one of nature's sculptures, a hidden grotto along the western Portuguese coast.

For the most part, the cave was dark and cold. Yet the

sand, which was warmed by the solitary shaft of light, chased the chill from her body. Trish sat down and watched the dark water wash away her footprints at the edge of the tiny beach. She cupped her hands and called out. The walls reverberated with a familiar echo until she was left with the lapping sound of another wave.

The water's edge drew closer and traces of her footprints were erased. She stayed there a long time. The water touched her feet; little of the beach remained. Soon it would be gone.

17

❧❧

It was a Sunday morning in July. Phillip could have been at the beach, his friends were, but he had other plans. He sped along Route 18 in central Jersey. A blur of beige and brown three-story dwellings was to his left, followed by a large white sign with black letters informing all passersby that this was part of Douglass—The State Women's College. To his right was a long red boat house perched on the banks of the Raritan River. A gift of the Class of 1916, it held the racing sculls for the Rutgers University crew team. Soon the highway split. Taking the left fork, he crossed Easton Avenue and turned into a complex of garden apartments. He eased in front of 18J.

There were hundreds of attached residences, duplexes, which were indistinguishable from one another. Each had its own postage-size patch of grass in front of it. The red brick walls had turned brown from years of beating rain and melting snow. Once white shutters were now smeared and blotched. The metal netting on the front door screen had been frequently patched, but now, a piece lifted from the chipped molding. Someone had neglected to fix it. The trim was in need of paint and overgrown rhododendrons blocked the front windows. A dead azalea bush, long past resuscitating, was in the corner.

Faded window shades were halfway down, blocking the late afternoon sun. An attic exhaust fan hummed, trying to coax the stifling heat from the apartment. Phillip saw movement through the door. Whoever was coming, walked slowly.

"Excuse me, ma'am," Phillip said hoping he rang the wrong door. The woman was stooped and had a lone hair growing from a dark mole on her cheek. "Do the Rudermans live here?"

"May I help you?" She was formless in a plain powder blue dress that reminded him of a grandmother . . . anybody's grandmother. Esther Ruderman wore no makeup and had the pale skin of a winter's hibernation. Her dull, lifeless hair needed to be combed. Dark hollows housed her eyes.

"May I help you," she said again.

"Uh, I guess so. My name is Phillip Hunter and. . . ." He stood telling this stranger about blood types, Ezekial Johnson, and the list of names from a hospital nursery eighteen years ago. At first he talked rapidly, but when she tilted her head and creases formed in the corners of her eyes from smiles of long ago, he slowed down. His even and steady voice got higher and his hands waved when he described Mrs. Schwartz. And he laughed picturing Mr. Lantelli missing the basket.

"That's quite a story, Phillip. Are you thirsty? Come inside and I'll get you a cold drink. I'm sure my Morris would like to meet you."

Smells of freshly baked apple pie spread from the kitchen, giving life to an otherwise dreary living room. She motioned him to sit on the sofa bought thirty years earlier; either the cushions had been reupholstered or anyone rarely sat on them. The couch might have been new except the peach fabric was faded where the sun used to wash it, when light was a welcomed guest.

In celebration of the unexpected visitor, her gnarled fingers negotiated the rotary knob of the mogul socket on the floor lamp. The chiffon silk shade cast a yellow hue, creating long shadows on empty walls. He could see the mahogany dining room table, with its ball-and-claw carved legs stretched to the floor in Chippendale elegance, out of place with the rest of the furnishings. A lonely wooden hutch with cut-crystal panels was filled with dishes; they had the same multi-colored stemware Mrs. Lantelli had. Together, the Rudermans and Lantellis had service for twelve. An ashtray was proudly displayed from Las Vegas on an end table, and atop the Philco television were two dolls of Amish farmers and the Eiffel Tower, mementos from trips they no longer took.

Morris Ruderman came down the stairs. He had a pockmarked face with a jowl under his chin, and a large nose which was off to one side. Maybe he had been a boxer. What little was left of his hair was pure white. His belly was draped in a ribbed, white, tank-top tee-shirt, the kind with straps and no sleeves. He wore baggy green shorts and black, knee-high Banlon socks with blue boat deck sneakers. "Hi!" he said walking over to Phillip. His soft gray eyes and two-handed handshake were comforting.

"Morris, dear, please take a seat. This nice young man has something to tell you." Phillip sipped apple juice. He felt the cool liquid slide down his throat and hit his stomach, making a sloshing sound that only he could hear. He cleared his throat and began. As he spoke, their eyes never strayed from his.

They continued to stare after he finished, like wax figures in a museum. Had they heard him?

He cleared his throat.

"In order for me to find my parents, I need to know your blood types."

Still no response.

"Do you know them?"

"Know what?" Esther asked.

"Of course we do, Phillip." Morris took over. "Recently, my wife had an operation, so we know our blood types." Phillip dared not breathe. He pictured Morris a slow driver; he probably wore a hat! "I'm Type A and my wife is AB . . . or is it the other way around?"

"No, you have it right, Morris. Does that help you?"

The room grew small.

"Maybe." Phillip wiped his forehead with a paper napkin. "You have to be tested at the Essex County Blood Center. Would you go?"

"We'd be pleased to go," Morris Ruderman said, putting his arm around his wife. Phillip wrote down the directions.

"I can do that," Morris said.

"Do what?" Phillip asked.

"Write backwards."

"Oh, I do it without thinking."

"Me, too."

Phillip turned to leave. On the way out, he noticed a picture hidden behind the opened front door. It was their son. Phillip moved the door to see better. The boy in the picture looked to be the same age as Todd. He was angular with dark, straight hair. He stood in a driveway. There was a basketball pole to one side and a bicycle leaning against the garage door.

Ari Ruderman looked like Ron. Side-by-side, they would be dead ringers. Phillip's ears rang and his tongue swelled.

"It was taken when he was fourteen," said Morris.

"When will he be home? I'd like to meet him."

"That was our last picture," Morris's voice drifted. "Ari was killed that summer when a truck crashed into him. He was riding his bicycle. That was four years ago."

"He was our only baby." Esther slipped from Morris's grasp and fell into the nearby club chair. Morris nodded. "She does it a lot," his eyes explained.

"I'm so sorry. I didn't know."

"How could you?" Morris replied. "I'm sure you're a good boy—just like Ari was. We'll see you at the lab."

Morris all but shoved Phillip out the door. He kneeled in front of Esther and cradled her heaving head. Morris squeezed his eyelids and bit his lip, and wondered if the pain would ever stop.

18

♦♦

The Bellmans lived in a shingled three-bedroom house on Shadowbrook Drive. A large redwood deck that obscured most of the backyard, was trimmed with rectangular flower boxes filled with hundreds of red, yellow, and orange nasturtium. A red-checkered plastic drape covered a table laden with the trimmings of a Sunday summer feast—assorted salads, pickles, chips, and ears of baby-white corn from a local farmer's market.

Decked out in a white chef's hat and apron, Frank sang out loud while basting chicken parts with his special sauce. "As long as you don't come within ten feet of the barbecue," he once told Myrna, "our marriage will last forever." That was easy enough, she hated cooking.

"Mrs. Bellman, thank you for inviting me to dinner," Gillian said. "Anything I can do to help?"

"Thanks, Gillian, everything's under control—that is, if Chef Frank avoids burning the chicken. How's your summer been?"

She flexed her right biceps.

"Impressive," Myrna squeezed Gillian's arm, "don't let the fellas see it, they'll be jealous."

"It's the main advantage of scooping ice cream."

"What's the other?"

"Getting nauseous at the thought of chunky almond fudge." They laughed. "Actually, I'm lucky to get a job, lots of kids couldn't find anything this year. Besides, it's a no-brainer, that's why I took a writing course."

"Phillip told me you were. How do you like it?"

"It's the best. We do a novella each week and then the teacher gives us an exercise that we read to the class. So far we've read Conrad, Flaubert, and Thomas Mann. I thought I wanted to be a psych major but writing's looking pretty good."

"By the time you've finished U of P, you'll change majors again, everyone does."

"I'm not so sure. Literature has opened up a whole new world for me. The idea of creating something from nothing, of putting words together like a painter so people see and feel what I do is such a turn on."

"Gillian, you have to be passionate about it; writing doesn't put a lot of money in your bank account."

"I'd rather be happy and fulfilled."

"Well, you've got the right spirit."

"Come and get it," Frank yelled.

"Let's hope something's left," Myrna said taking Gillian by the arm.

After Todd, everyone extended their plate, marching past the cook, selecting a favorite piece. Todd started eating before everyone was seated, and Ron smacked him.

"What was that for?"

"Being a pig. Don't you have any manners? Frank hasn't sat down yet."

"You don't have to hit me."

147

"I didn't hit you. It was a love tap. If I'd hit you, you would have known it."

"So this is what it's like having brothers; it's kind of cool," Kevin Bellman said.

Myrna saw Todd's arm poised to return the 'love tap.'

"Ron, how're you boys enjoying the summer?" she asked.

"It's been okay," he answered. "Playing baseball every day."

"I thought you loved baseball."

"I do, but not when it's hot."

"And what about you, Todd?"

"Fine." That's what Todd usually said. He was partially hidden by a rapidly growing pile of chicken bones.

"Are you going to college?" Ron asked Kevin.

"Nope."

"Everybody goes to college," said Todd.

"Not my bag. Can't be bothered with books 'n stuff like that. Besides, I got it all figured out. Gonna save me some money and get my own station. Not one of those Jiffy Lube franchises. That's for jerks. I'm gonna specialize in customizing them Jap and German cars. That's where the money's at."

They stayed outside until mosquitoes overran the blue bug light, which zapped nonstop for the last hour.

"The bugs are getting pretty bad. Let's have dessert in the dining room," Myrna said. Phillip lagged behind.

"Aunt Myrna?"

"Yes?"

"This morning I found the Rudermans. They're the ones. I'm sure of it."

The screen door slid open, Frank was carrying the serving platter with a lone chicken wing.

"Is this private?"

"It's the Rudermans, Uncle Frank," Phillip said. "One is AB and the other's A. The blood types are right and he's dyslexic, too. He writes mirror-image, same way I do. But the clincher was their son's picture. He looked exactly like Ron."

"What do you mean looked? Didn't you meet him?"

"No, he was killed by a truck four years ago."

"Those poor people. Did they agree to the tests?"

"Yup. I gave them Pat Novick's address. They're going tomorrow." Phillip looked from one to the other. "Can I ask you guys a huge favor?"

"Anything, Phil," Frank said.

"Would one of you come to the Blood Bank tomorrow?"

"We'll be there, Phillip," Myrna said, throwing her arms around him and hugging him tightly. "You better believe we'll be there."

Myrna got there first. She waved when she saw Frank and Phillip drive into the Blood Bank's parking lot. Together, they walked into the tobacco-colored, brick and glass building. They were early and Phillip wondered when the Rudermans would arrive. But Morris and Esther were already sitting motionless on the plastic contoured chairs in the reception area. Pat Novick greeted the latest arrivals.

"Everyone seems anxious, which explains why all of you got here early," he smiled like a television game show host. He had sun-streaked hair from playing golf three times a week, and wore white cotton slacks, wooden clogs, and an open-collared lavender Polo shirt that revealed a chest full of honey-colored hair. A copper bracelet jangled from his wrist.

"We get to places early." Morris rose from his seat. "How are you, Phillip?" Phillip introduced his aunt and uncle, and

149

then the lab director escorted the Rudermans to a back operatory. He drew and labeled the blood himself. No one spoke. With telltale Band-Aids in place, arms bent, they returned to the reception area.

While everyone settled in, Dr. Novick inserted the specimens into the computerized Coulter analyzer, grasping each tube firmly. When he finished, he returned to the reception area. Aware everyone was staring at him, or the floor, or their hands, he felt obliged to explain what was happening to the blood samples.

". . . so you see, there are numerous blood proteins that form a genetic blueprint for each person. Many are named after their discoverers, like Kell, Cellano, Coombs, Hegeman, DeFalco, and others. Separately, they do not mean very much but as a group, these proteins form a unique combination for every individual on this planet. It's an infallible means of identifying people—and offspring."

He'd seen expressionless faces like theirs many times before at lectures and lab demonstrations. Patients rarely wanted to hear details. They assumed he knew what he was doing if for no other reasons than that he wore a white coat, and *doctor* preceded his name. He saw Phillip listen. Morris did, too.

". . . and the day has come when we can create *designer genes!*" It was his favorite line, a sure winner! But no one laughed. Phillip's lip twitched, but that was it. Knowing he'd lost his audience, he returned to his desk to tackle a mound of paperwork. The computerized hi-tech verdict would be rendered in thirty minutes.

Absolute silence filled the room. Some stared, others read. Time ticked away seconds. The stillness was punctuated by a turning page, a cough, a deep breath, or a sigh.

Then a shrill bell pierced the air. Everyone's head

whipped in unison and watched Pat Novick reenter the room, running his fingers through his golden hair. He read the results out loud. "Positive, negative, positive, positive, negative, negative, negative, positive, negative . . ." the printout analyzed the presence or absence of each protein. He compared these results to the ones obtained from Frank's experiment. Still silence. The suspense mounted as he looked from printout to printout, face to face. His hands plunged to his sides as he said, "It's a match."

Everyone looked at Phillip, but he did nothing—he was frozen in place. Ever since that first day at the Beth, the same question had been running through his mind: Who was he?

Shuffling feet brought him in front of Morris and Esther. Esther grabbed his hands and kissed each one.

"Phillip, this is very confusing. You should be with your relatives. Maybe we could talk later this week."

Morris took Esther by the arm.

Phillip didn't consciously form the words but he heard himself say good-bye. The glass door opened and closed and he watched the Rudermans get into an ancient turquoise Olds Ninety-eight, one that had survived oil embargos and high gas prices, one that he imagined gave stability to their lives.

Driving home, the Rudermans didn't talk much. Esther had fallen asleep, and Morris let his mind drift to the moment he first cast his eyes on her. Life had been lonely after the Korean War. Without a trade or a college education, Morris became a salesman whose nondescript face, except for a crooked nose, left no lasting impression on anyone, especially young women.

151

She had come in with two friends who might have been prettier but he never noticed. He only had eyes for her. It was summertime and her cotton dress revealed a trim figure beneath it. They tried on many shoes and he hoped Esther would express gratitude for his help but she left without saying a word.

Months passed. Morris jerked his head every time a customer stepped on the welcome mat connected to the hidden chime. He yearned to meet the mysterious woman but she never returned.

Summer turned into winter. Morris regularly went to Branch Brook Park because he enjoyed watching the girls ice-skate. He liked to watch their short skirts lift as they twirled, revealing beige stockinged thighs. He was thinner then, and had been an expert skater. With hands clasped behind him, he smoked his pipe and glided across the ice. He circled for the hundredth time that afternoon when he saw her step onto the ice. His heart leaped so high his feet joined it and he ended up on the ice. Luckily, she didn't see him fall.

Morris picked himself up, determined not to let this opportunity slip away. He aimed to dazzle her, speeding in front of her and then skating backwards, culminating in a graceful series of concentric circles. Yet she talked with her friends, not noticing him. On the next go 'round, he became bolder, he jumped and spun at center ice, all to no avail. He threw his hands up in frustration; what did he have to do to get her attention? And then it occurred to him!

Morris helped her get up, apologizing profusely for his clumsiness. He was glad she wasn't hurt and when she thanked him for his concern he invited her for hot chocolate. What a fateful day it had been! Afterward, they met each week until the warm weather made the ice unsafe. By then,

152

their hearts had blossomed with the emerging daffodils and crocuses and they were soon married.

With the responsibility of a new bride and the family that would surely be on its way, Morris took his meager savings and with the help of a G.I. mortgage, bought a house. He worked harder and harder in the shoe store and was silently relieved when Mr. Shapiro got rid of the x-ray machine that allowed customers to see their feet through the shoes they tried on.

He and Esther were happy together. They had everything they could ever hope for except the one thing that never came: Esther was barren. She was a teacher and the more time she spent around children, the more painful her fate became to her.

Having barely adjusted to life's unfairness, they were shocked when Ari Kenneth entered their lives. Esther had felt nauseous and thought she had food poisoning. Her doctor told her otherwise, giving her news that was much easier to digest.

Ari was special from the beginning, lighting up a room with his shining face. He asked lots of questions and read anything he could get his hands on. Teachers loved him. Morris and Esther adored him. He was their life.

Now Esther hummed while doing the laundry and sang lullabies when she put Ari to bed. Morris sent flowers celebrating the day they met on the ice and showered Esther with presents on each birthday and every holiday he could think of.

But carousels stop turning, music ends, and flowers wither and die. Ari had been riding his bike home from Randy Bressman's house, when the drunken driver of an eighteen wheeler hit Ari and threw him 25 feet in the air.

153

Morris turned off the Turnpike at Exit 9. A light mist fell and he drove carefully. He entered their apartment complex, still longing for their old house, his house, the one Esther made him sell. She said every room was a reminder that a child would no longer fill it with laughter. Nothing was the same after Ari was gone—they simply tolerated life.

After the Rudermans drove away, Pat Novick let Phillip use his private office.

"Phillip, repeat what you just said. This static's terrible. You found what?" Trish strained to make sense from the garbled words. They had another day to their vacation and hadn't expected a phone call from home.

"I . . . said . . . I . . . found . . . my . . . biological parents. It . . . was . . . the . . . Rudermans."

"Wait while I get your father," she snapped her fingers to get Brad's attention. With the receiver between their ears, Phillip repeated the tale about meeting Morris and Esther. He didn't mention that Ari Ruderman had died, and in the excitement, Brad and Trish didn't ask about him. Brad took the receiver.

"Are you all right, son?"

"I guess so. I feel weird, kind of disoriented. I'll be okay."

"Hang in there, Phillip, we'll be home before you know it. Everything will be just fine."

"I know it will, Dad. Bye." Phillip disconnected the call but still held the phone, as if touching it linked him to his parents. Moments ago, he was Phillip Hunter. His life was in order. Now everything seemed different.

Frank and Myrna had waited.

"Frank, I need to tell Gillian. I'll come to work later."

"You take all the time you need," said Myrna. "Tonight, have dinner with us again. Bring the boys."

Phillip found Gillian leaning into the freezer, struggling to reach a near-empty container of chocolate ice cream. Almost falling into the case, she lifted the cardboard drum and eked out two scoops for the anxious woman, whose pudgy fingers couldn't wait to grab the pre-lunch treat. Gillian's face lit up when she saw Phillip come in.

"Hey! What're you doing here?"

"Can you take a break?"

Gillian shook her head.

"Can't. The manager went to make a deposit, I'm alone. We can talk until he gets back."

He stood the full measure of his six feet.

"I found them."

"Who?"

"My BPs."

"Tell me, tell me! The Rudermans?"

"Yup."

"Are you okay?"

"I think so. But what am I going to do?"

"What do you mean?"

"What am I going to do about the Rudermans? I thought this was a great idea, but now I'm not sure."

"Phillip, you don't have to do anything. You wanted to find them and you did. You satisfied your curiosity, now it's finished."

"That's what I thought was going to happen, but I'm not so sure, Gilly."

The door clanged and a customer came in. While Gillian went to satisfy another watering mouth, Phillip walked around the store. There was a community bulletin board with notices of Livingston's 10K race on Labor Day, St. Philomena's Annual Summer Carnival, an apartment sublet across from West Essex General Hospital, and a poster of missing children. He studied their innocent smiles. Was it the last time they were happy? They reminded him of Ari's picture on the wall.

"Phil? Phil? Earth to Phil?"

"Sorry. I was a million miles away. These pictures got to me."

"Yeah. They change them every few weeks. Isn't it horrible not to know what happens to your kid? Anyway, your BPs may be nice people but you don't owe them anything. They didn't raise you. You have no history with them. They . . . well, they're just two people you happened to meet."

"Yeah, and their son, who really belonged to my parents, just happens to be dead."

"He's dead? That's horrible!"

"He was hit by a truck four years ago . . . and he was their only child. Their lives are so empty now."

"You can't look at it that way. They had fourteen good years with him. They raised him and loved him thinking he was theirs. That makes him theirs." She reached out to touch his arm.

"They seemed so sad."

"Of course they would. What's worse than burying a child? But it's their loss, not yours. Don't get weird on me, Phillip. You've got great parents and fabulous brothers. . . ."

"Who? Ron and Todd? They're fabulous when they're sleeping."

"Get off it, you're so lucky. I wish I had siblings. You've got everything going for you—looks, brains, a great future and. . . ."

"And you. I know I'm lucky, and I'm grateful for everything I have. I really am. But they looked so. . . ."

Just then, her manager returned. Gillian circled behind the counter and blew Phillip a kiss as he left.

A day had come and gone, and Brad and Trish were due to arrive that afternoon. Phillip hoisted amber tinted reagent jugs onto a shelf, recalling yesterday's phone call to Morris.

"Hello. This is Phillip . . . Phillip Hunter."

"Phillip? We were just talking about you. The missus is a little under the weather from yesterday's excitement. Nothing serious. So how are you?"

"A little tired, myself."

"Where are you calling from, Phillip?"

"From work. I just wanted to say hello. I called my folks and told them. They're coming back tomorrow."

"You called all the way to Portugal? I bet they were surprised to hear from you?"

"That's an understatement."

"So what did you say?"

"That you and Esther were nice."

"Thank you, Phillip. I'd like to meet them one day."

"Sure. Gotta go now. Bye, Morris."

"Good-bye, Phillip."

Finished, he reached for a rack of test tubes when all of a sudden he looked up and saw Brad and Trish standing in the lab doorway. Nearly breaking the glassware, Phillip sprinted to them and lifted his mother off her feet.

"I missed you so much, Phillip."

"Not as much as I missed you, Mom." He kissed her again then put her down and mauled his father in a giant bear hug.

"Welcome home," Frank called to Trish and Brad. "I'll catch up on your trip later, but I think you and Phillip have a lot to talk about. You can use my office."

"Did you ever get to Winfield Arlen Jones?" Brad asked as they sat down.

"You got to hear this," Phillip studied their reactions. "I drive up to this beautiful mansion, you know the kind they'd put on 'Lifestyles of the Rich and Famous,' and this English butler announces me to Mr. Jones. Now get this," Phillip broke out laughing, "the dude comes out in a riding outfit wearing one of those little black riding caps. I took one look and knew who he was."

"Is he in finances? Maybe he's a banker," said Trish.

"Nope. It was Arlen James, you know, the black comedian. Todd and Ron watch him on all those HBO comedy hours. Seems that Arlen James is only a stage name. When I saw him, I had the hardest time keeping a straight face. But he was real nice, he invited me to come back to meet his son."

"Speaking of which, what kind of kid is the Ruderman's son?" Brad asked.

Phillip's smile vanished.

"What's the matter?" asked Brad.

"Is there something wrong with him? Is he handicapped? He's not crippled or Mongoloid, is he?"

"No, Mom, it's worse. I don't know how to tell you this. Ari's dead. He was run over by a truck."

Brad grabbed Trish's hand but she pulled away.

"That's too bad," she said. "I'm sorry for them but it makes it a lot easier for us. I guess the book's closed now."

Brad clamped his hands around his scalp. "Christ, I can't believe you. Phillip's just told us we lost a son and you're fucking relieved. What's wrong with you?"

Trish locked into Phillip's eyes.

"Phillip, ever since this sordid mess began, I wanted no part of it. You're my son, not Ari. I can't have feelings for a child I've never seen. I certainly can't be expected to miss

158

him, or feel a loss now that I know what happened to him."

"All I know is I wanted to meet him, and now I can't," Brad muttered. Trish ignored his remark and continued.

"Phillip, nothing's changed between you and me. Your father has to learn that bringing a child up in the world is what parenting's all about. That's why adopted kids are loved and stepchildren can be nurtured by parents not biologically related to them."

"I know what you're saying is right, Mom. I don't have any special feeling for the Rudermans, but, I hope you don't get mad at me: I invited them for Sunday dinner. I don't know why I did it."

"Why do I have to cook for them? They're nothing to me."

"For Chrissakes, Trish, stop thinking about yourself. It was a nice gesture on Phillip's part, and besides, there's no harm in meeting these people."

19

❦❦

Brad and Trish left Phillip. They rode the elevator to the main floor, each deep in thought. Before exiting the sprawling drug company, they waited for a paunchy man wearing an open-colored white shirt and blue pants, to get clear of the revolving lobby door.

"Do you know where Dr. Bellman's laboratory is?" he asked.

"Take the elevator to the third floor and turn left," Brad answered, "you can't miss it."

"Thank you." His rubber soles squeaked on the polished granite floor.

Upstairs, Frank returned to his lab to find Brad and Trish had gone. "I bet it felt good to see your parents."

"I didn't know I could miss them that much. It's been some week!"

"I'll say. Three days ago you found the Rudermans; the next day blood tests confirmed they were your BPs. Now your real parents are back. That qualifies as *excitement.*"

Polite knuckles tapped the door frame.

"Mr. Ruderman, what are you doing here?" Phillip asked. "You just missed my parents."

"They must've been the nice couple I asked for directions.

Forgive me for barging in this way, but I was in the neighborhood and wanted to see where you worked. I'm sorry I didn't call first."

"It's not a problem. Glad you could stop by," said Phillip. It occurred to him that until minutes earlier, his own father hadn't visited the lab.

"Phillip, why don't you give Mr. Ruderman the ten dollar tour," Frank said.

"Good idea. Let's go, Mr. Ruderman."

"Morris. Please call me Morris."

"Okay . . . Morris. The tour begins this way." Phillip sprang into the lab only to hear telltale squeaks plod behind him. Phillip came to know that Morris had one pace that came from years of walking back and forth, carrying tens of thousands of shoe boxes. Phillip introduced him to Soo and Dr. Sims. He showed Morris the animal cages and the light microscope. He was about to demonstrate the electron microscope when Morris muttered something about "Esther's waiting." Excusing himself, he left before Phillip could ask a question.

Tommy Donovan's freckles danced when he saw Brad. "Back so soon, Boss? You could've unpacked, the building's still here."

"I can see that, Tommy. Were there any problems?"

"Nothing I couldn't handle. The new catalogue's a big hit. We got the sockets, and the importers notified us that the musical chips left Kyoto."

"When will they get here?" Brad asked.

"Two weeks. Got back orders up the wazzoo for them."

"I hope we ordered enough."

"Are you kidding, Boss? You ordered millions!"

"Tommy, you can never have enough of a good thing."

* * *

Trish felt awkward returning to work after she had poured her heart out to Steve before going to Portugal. She remembered the strange feeling that overcame her as she spoke to him—a bond that had never existed before. She remembered how she felt when his hands were on her shoulders, her cheek on his chest. Phillip wasn't the only one she had thought about in the grotto.

"I didn't expect you until tomorrow. When did your plane arrive?" Steve Sadler asked passing her desk.

"I would've been here sooner but we ran to see Phillip."

"How is he?"

"Considering he found his biological parents while we were gone, he's fine."

"Jesus Christ! He really found them!" He rattled the steel filing cabinet. "What are you going to do?"

"Nothing, what can I do? It's too late to change anything. And after Sunday's dinner, Phillip invited them with Brad's blessing, I hope to never see or hear about them again."

Steve issued a low whistle. "Why have them in your house? What purpose will that serve?"

"Exactly what I told Brad." She measured the pile of papers on her desk. "I'm not sure it was worth taking a vacation."

"I'm glad you're back, Trish. The office was quiet without you."

"I don't make that much noise, Steve. You never missed me before."

Two hours later, her desk was less cluttered. At least that part of her life would be straight the next day. Trish applied fresh lipstick. She was putting the cloisonne holder away, a memento from a Parisian vacation, when Steve popped into her office.

"Do you need to go home right away?"

"Actually, I do." She couldn't wait to see Ron and Todd

and experience a usual chaotic dinner. If Todd wasn't late from pre-season football practice, then Ron would be at a friend's house; if Ron wasn't playing baseball, then Phillip was with Gillian. Someone always had something to do and now, Phillip would be going off to Cornell in five weeks.

"I wondered how you were feeling. After all, when you left there were a lot of emotions flying between us." Trish looked down.

"I have to go, I can't deal with this now."

Steve blocked the door. With uncertain steps, Trish approached. They were nose to nose. She smelled his minty breath. With the faintest touch, she edged past him, feeling his magnetic stare on her back. She did not dare turn around for fear he would ask her to stay.

Sunday came too quickly for the Hunters. Brad barely slept. When he finally awoke, he was surprised to find Trish missing. She had been up since dawn, going to the market and bakery, getting the necessary things for dinner. Brad tried to busy himself weeding the flower beds around the house, but nothing helped. He took a walk, read the paper, trimmed a hedge and was exhausted by the time Phillip warned him the Rudermans would come early.

"I better get ready then," and he lumbered up the stairs and turned the Thermisol switch to twenty minutes. Steam would fill the airtight stall, which doubled as a sauna, in eight minutes. Brad eased into the haze; the heat burned his nostrils. He rested his forehead on the tiled wall and let the pulsating water blast his back. He knew it didn't do much good but it made him feel better.

And then without warning, his knees bent and his chest began to heave. The already saturated air made it difficult to breathe. He crumpled to the rubber floor and covered his eyes.

163

He was always the strong macho man. No one ever told him about how the loss he would feel—the emptiness for a son he held once but would never hold again. Why didn't Trish feel it? Brad wondered if Ari could have snagged a ball or caught fish with Phillip's joy. Had Trish been right all along, that his drive to find their biological son had been a mistake? When was the last time they made love?

The scalding water pelted his skin, yet Brad was covered with goose bumps. His body quaked. Did what happened eighteen years ago truly matter anymore?

❦❦

20

P hillip picked up Gillian.

"What're they like?" Gillian asked on the ride back to his house.

"It's hard to say. Mrs. Ruderman doesn't talk much. She kind of sits and looks around. Morris runs the show."

"Do you like her?"

"She's okay, I guess."

"And Morris?"

"I like him a lot. He shakes with two hands and there's always a twinkle in his eye. I bet he was a practical joker as a kid."

They got to the house minutes before the doorbell rang.

Trish stopped in front of the mirror one last time. She wore a fawn silk blouse and navy skirt cut just above the knee, an outfit suited for work. Not a hair out of place, she took a deep breath and strutted down the stairs.

Brad talked with them in the vestibule. Morris and Esther were flushed. Their clothes were wrinkled with damp circles in unflattering places. A drop or two of sweat fell from their chins onto the ceramic-tiled floor.

"You should have tested the air conditioner, Morris."

"You always tell me the car's too cool and then start

sneezing. Who knew it would be such a scorcher?"

"Hi! I'm Trish Hunter. So glad you could make it."

"It's a pleasure to meet you, Mrs. Hunter," Morris said, grabbing her hand in his double-grip fashion.

"Me, too."

"Brad, why don't you get the Rudermans something to drink. I'm sure everyone could use one." Brad got Morris a scotch on the rocks and Esther a Perrier instead of the seltzer she had wanted.

"Let's go out back, it's quite cool there." Trish ushered them onto the deck off the kitchen where hors d'oeuvres had been already placed: vegetable crudités, onion dip, potato chips, and pretzels.

Phillip spun around when he heard the glass door slide. "Hi!"

"Hey, it's good to see you again," Morris said pumping away. After introductions to Ron, Todd, and Gillian were made, they nibbled and drank under the shade of a large tulip poplar that shielded them from the late afternoon sun. A breeze blew through the tree-filled yard, and Esther's grim pallor soon gave way to a rosy freshness.

"Get this, Trish. Morris and I lived two blocks apart in Newark. It is such a small world. I guess it's true that we're all separated by six degrees."

"Sometimes, I think we're two people removed from each other," said Morris. "Do you remember Mr. Brewer from Maple Avenue?"

"Old brewery face? I held my breath every time he got near the band saw. There wasn't a day I didn't think he'd lose a finger."

"Did he still. . . . ?" Morris tipped his hand.

"Drink tea? Constantly. Phillip, get a load of this," Brad said. "This Mr. Brewer was the wood shop teacher. He used to drink tea all day long from a red thermos. I thought he

166

was gutsy because teachers never ate in class. Anyway, one day, he left the cap off and I smelled it."

"Whiskey!" Morris roared, thrusting his drink to the sky. "The bastard never changed!" Morris heaved so hard, he nearly fell off his chair; everyone laughed.

"And do you remember Mrs. Tarsson?" Brad asked, wiping the tears from his eyes.

"The midget music teacher? She'd be standing and still couldn't see you talking in the back."

"She wasn't a midget, Morris, she was a dwarf," Brad said. Phillip poked Gillian in the ribs.

"They sound like us talking about our teachers."

"Phillip, it may come as a surprise, but your father and I were once young."

"Who's hungry?" asked Trish. "I hope salmon's fine. We weren't sure what you'd like."

"Salmon is perfect," Morris said. Esther smiled in agreement.

Dinner was a success: a salad of summer greens, grilled salmon filets with dijon mustard sauce, asparagus vinaigrette, and wild brown rice, completed with fresh fruit, vanilla ice cream with a cookie wafer embellishing it, and key lime pie. Earlier, Trish had warned Ron and Todd, who rarely ate fish, to "enjoy" it. They did the best they could, moving it around so it appeared they had eaten enough.

"Who else did you meet on the Newark Bears?" Ron asked.

"Besides Berra and Rizzuto? I remember seeing Duke Snider and Don Newcombe play for the Montreal Royals. That '48 Royal team was one of the greatest!"

"That must've been awesome."

Trish saw Todd finish his second helping of desserts.

"Boys, dinner is over. You may be excused." As if a starter's gun had been fired, Ron and Todd scrambled from their chairs, said their farewells, and bolted to change clothes so they could play ball. Trish caught Brad's attention and nodded to the liquor cabinet.

"Uh, who wants an after dinner drink?" Brad asked.

Esther leaned forward.

"Thank you for a wonderful dinner."

"You're welcome, Esther."

"I need to ask one question."

"Yes?"

"Are you Jewish?" Trish shot Brad a shocked look.

"We're not. Why do you ask?"

"We didn't think you were," Morris said. "It would've been a lot easier."

"Easier? Easier for whom?" Brad asked.

Phillip shrugged to Gillian, he had no idea what this was about.

"To tell you the truth, there's a problem."

"Morris, what does Jewish have to do with anything?" Trish asked.

The white-haired man used his open palm to wipe away the wetness that had formed on his lips.

"My dear Hunters, we raised a Jewish son. Ari was circumcised according to Jewish tradition, went to religious school, and had a Bar Mitzvah at thirteen."

"We know about those things," Brad said. "So what's the problem?"

"The problem is he's buried in a Jewish cemetery."

"Where else would you bury him?" Trish asked.

Morris clasped his large hands together, one palm in the other. His barrel chest collapsed as he blurted the truth.

"Ari was never Jewish."

"You did all those Jewish things. Of course he was Jewish, what else could he have been?"

"Anything but Jewish. To be Jewish, Mrs. Hunter, one

must have a Jewish mother. It's been that way since the time of Moses." Morris's gray eyes met Trish's. "You are not Jewish."

"Esther's Jewish," Trish said.

"Yes she is, and that's how we raised him. But the rabbis don't look at it that way. According to Talmudic Law, Ari was a gentile."

"Even so, why would it matter now? Ari's been dead over four years," Brad said.

"Dad, I think I know. Only Jews can be buried in a Jewish cemetery. That means Ari doesn't belong there. Right, Morris?"

"How do you know that, Phillip?"

"One of my friends, Len Ginsberg, came to school all upset. His mother had converted to Judaism and when she died, they wanted to bury her in the family plot, next to his grandparents. But the rabbi, who was Orthodox, wouldn't do it because he said she really wasn't Jewish."

"What'd they do?" Trish asked.

"Buried her in a Christian cemetery," Morris said.

"Yup."

"You see, the only sacred ground in the Jewish religion is a cemetery and only Jews are permitted to be buried there. Even the land temples are built on is not considered sacred. Nowadays, because of all the intermarriages, some husbands and wives are separated when they die."

"It's a terrible thing," said Esther.

"So Ari's not supposed to be there?" Brad said.

Morris nodded. Gillian's eyes widened.

"Does he have to be . . . dug up?" Trish asked, her voice tailing off.

"I've thought about this a great deal and I think, no I know, the best thing to do is forget about it."

"Can you do that?" Brad asked.

"Technically not, but who's going to tell?"

"But if it's wrong. . . ."

"Brad, it's not a question of right or wrong, it's a question of what's good for Ari. Let him rest in peace."

"I agree, Morris, but you said yourself. . . ." Morris held his finger up, like Joseph Lantelli had once done.

"Brad, listen to me. There are times when one has to know when *not* to do something. This is one of those times."

"Enough talk about cemeteries," Esther said. "Do you want to see a picture?"

"A what?" A corner of Trish's lip turned up, her forehead creased.

"A picture. A picture of Ari."

"Uh . . . sure I do," Trish said and reached for the laminated print. "Jesus." Trish passed it to Brad like a hot potato. He studied it for a long while, his hand supporting his chin like a Rodin model. He handed it back. There was nothing to say.

Morris suggested it was time to leave. Everyone agreed.

The Rudermans said their thank yous and good-byes. Brad walked them to their car and reviewed the directions back to the Turnpike. He stood there until their turquoise tank disappeared.

Brad returned to find the kitchen empty. When he entered his bedroom, he saw Trish face down, the bed shaking.

"Trish? What's wrong, honey?"

"He's dead! He's dead! Who I saw in that picture was our boy . . . it wasn't real before."

"Honey, I felt the same way. Look," Brad said, wanting to comfort her, "we've had Phillip all these years. We still do. The Rudermans lost their son. Look how lucky we are. They don't have any children."

She blotted her eyes in the pillow case, leaving black smudges.

"Here."

She blew her nose.

"I feel empty."

"So do I," he said.

"How could you? I'm his mother. You'll never know. . . ."

"Don't give me that maternal stuff now. I love all our children the same way you do. Now you're the one getting bent out of shape for some kid you never saw. Besides, you said yourself, 'Phillip is our son.' "

"Leave it to you to put my feelings down. I can never count on you when I need support."

"Look, I'm not putting you down. We both lost a son. I was the one who pushed for the truth so I'm painfully aware of just how real this is."

She lifted her head and sneered. "Speaking of which, look how smart Morris is."

"Smart?"

"How he handled the cemetery thing. Once he found out the truth, *he* didn't make an issue of it. *He* left Ari alone."

"I couldn't do that." Brad lowered his head.

"I know. And look at the price we're paying."

21

🌷🌷

The new week ushered in heat and dry weather. A drought had been declared and its effects were seen everywhere. Filth and grime became commonplace. Lawns became seared, shrubs drooped and power reductions forced controlled brownouts. The stifling air caused ill-temper: drivers stopped yielding to pedestrians, clerks no longer offered customers assistance, and children irritated their parents more easily. Sometimes the sky threatened relief. Menacing clouds would roll in, followed by barrages of hail stones. There was even an occasional tornado, but never enough thirst-quenching water.

Morris had been sitting on his front steps, listening to the radio. The apartment was smoldering; they directed a 20-inch fan over buckets of ice to no avail. Night was fast approaching. Morris ignored the flies buzzing around the uncovered light bulb that jutted from the canopy above his head. Esther was taking a bath when he heard the phone ring.

"Hello?"

"Morris, it's Phillip."

"Ah, Phillip, how are you? I hope you are in an air-conditioned room."

"I am, Morris. Morris?"

"Yes, Phillip?"

"Could I visit you Saturday?"

"That would be all right. How about lunch? Say twelve-thirty. Bye, Phillip."

"Great! See you then. Bye, Morris."

It was nine o'clock. The call made, Phillip splashed water on his face and tickled his teeth with the soft-nylon toothbrush his dentist's stacked hygienist recommended. He had tried to stretch his neck to look down her white uniform but she shoved a mirror in his face so he could learn to do the scrub technique.

Leaving a trail of clothes, he plopped into bed. He reached for the book on his night table, Stephen King's *Pet Sematary,* and found the dog-eared page. . . .

> . . . *he knew it was a dream . . . but the smell . . . the smell was real. Pungent. His eyes were clamped tight but he could still see. He reached beyond the pillow. Groping fingers felt a loose string . . . pulled it closer. The smell got stronger . . . damp autumn leaves . . . decaying wood chips . . . musk. He clutched it to his chest. Soft. Lumpy. Don't let go. The smell. The smell. Dirt and oil. He stashed it under his pillow . . . for safe keeping. Fingers touched it. . . .*

The alarm went off. Phillip reached under his pillow but nothing was there. It couldn't have been a dream; the pungent odor assaulted his nostrils . . . like it did two thousand yesterdays ago . . . when he was twelve.

Dream or not, he needed to touch it. He searched his closet; at first he didn't see it. He rummaged through ancient board games and four-piece puzzles, Golden story books and broken Boy Scout projects. Sparks, like bolts between electrodes, zapped his fingertips when he snatched his per-

173

sonally autographed Reggie Jackson glove from the shelf and pressed it to his face; nothing smelled better in the whole world. Kite string held a hardball firmly in the pocket of the well-oiled mitt, preserving its shape.

He unraveled the cord and slipped his hand inside. He pounded the pocket. Not as much padding as he remembered. He smelled it! Kissed it! Phillip wrapped it carefully and replaced it on the shelf. Had Ari known how to break in a glove?

Saturday Phillip returned to Somerset and parked in back of Morris's Oldsmobile. The vinyl roof was torn and the hood ornament was missing.

"Come in, Phillip," Morris called when he heard the doorbell. "Any problems getting here?"

"Nope."

"I'll be right out," Esther called from the kitchen. Morris turned the three-way switch on the bronze floor lamp and light filled the room. Esther carried a colorful bowl of fruit, in stark contrast to her sallow complexion. She looked older than she had at last week's dinner. He watched her put it down with difficulty, holding her back as she straightened up.

"Is everything ready?" Morris asked.

"Everything's on the table. I'm going upstairs now." She looked at Phillip. "I hope you like lunch. If you don't, Morris can fix you something else." Esther mounted the stairs without another word.

The dining room table was set for two. She had never intended to join them. Morris took his usual seat. Putting on a skullcap, he mumbled strange words while holding a twisted loaf of bread in his hand. He finished with an "Amen," and cut a piece for both of them.

"Esther and I are thankful for every meal we have, Phillip.

Here, dip the bread in this honey. It's for sweet hopes and dreams." Like Morris, Phillip licked his fingers.

"Help yourself," Morris handed him a platter.

"I know what the lox is. What's the other stuff?"

"This is smoked sturgeon and this one is kippered salmon," he pointed to wedges of gray-white flesh and dull pink meat topped with crinkled brown skin fanned around layers of lox.

"Are they good?"

"Try some." Morris put a slice of each on Phillip's plate. Phillip put his nose to them.

"Don't smell it, eat it! Put them on the bagel." Phillip started. "No, no, no, not like that. Take a schmear, this is a schmear. . . ." Morris loaded gobs of creamed cheese onto a fresh bagel, "nice and thick, then pile the fish on. No points for neatness. You want to feel your teeth sink through the fish and get stuck in the creamed cheese." Morris topped his masterpiece with lox and placed it on Phillip's plate . . . next to the bagel he had made.

"Look at that baby."

Phillip compared the two; it was like a finger sandwich to an over-stuffed hero. His mouth stretched to take a bite.

"It's good," he said, barely able to speak.

"Does Morris know how to make a bagel or what? So tell me, have you heard the idea that all eighteen-year-olds should perform some sort of national service? Would you go?"

Phillip gulped orange juice to wash down a wad of food.

"It sounds like a good idea. Everybody should do something for their country. It'll give everyone a common experience. If they had it, I guess I'd go."

"We need to make everyone feel more patriotic. It used to be that wars made everyone good about this country, that we were proud to be Americans. But lately," Morris sighed, "the young people only want to know what's in it for them. No one cares that this is the freest place in the world and it's a privilege to live here."

"It's hard to feel that way, Morris, when the government lets people go hungry and homeless. My friends say that if the government doesn't care, why should they? My dad says we need a good war to get American going again."

"War never solved anything. I'm talking about using the youth of this country to rebuild the infrastructure, to get the ghettos cleaned up, to teach people how to read and comfort senior citizens in old age homes. There's so much to be done."

"My father says if we ever go to war again it will be against the Chinese, that it was a mistake to ever think the Russians were our enemy."

"Not the Japanese?"

"Nope, the Chinese."

"You love your dad, don't you?"

"Both my parents. I'm real lucky."

"You certainly are. More coffee?"

"No thanks. I better be going. Tell Esther everything was wonderful."

They walked to the door. Phillip felt Morris's arm around his back, his calloused fingers on his shoulder. When they got to his Jeep, a sudden breeze picked up, rustling Phillip's hair . . . or was it the faint touch of Morris's thickened fingers.

It was the same routine as the previous week: Esther met him at the door but excused herself after a few minutes. A strong aroma filled the apartment.

"Do I smell corned beef?"

"Homemade. You'll love it. Esther cooks it 'til it melts in your mouth, like butter. Plus she made Ari's favorite dish for you: kasha varnishkas."

176

"What's kasha varni . . . kas."

"Varnishkas. Kasha varnishkas. They're noodle bowties and buckwheat with sauteed onions thrown in."

Morris placed a plateful of steaming shtetl pasta and corned beef in front of him. He leaned over and smelled it.

"Spoon or fork?" asked Phillip.

"Fork."

He swallowed. "It's great. It's really great." When he finished, he asked for seconds.

After lunch, Morris asked Phillip if he'd like to see his favorite place. "It's only a few minutes by car."

Phillip clutched the leather armrest as Morris drove over the rickety Landings Lane Bridge that he passed each time he visited the Rudermans. Built in 1895 at the narrowest juncture of the Raritan River, it was designed for horse and buggies, not steel chariots. Midway across the aged planking, Morris twisted and pointed over Phillip's shoulder to a thin ribbon of water choked by overgrown plants.

"That's what's left of the canal that used to connect New Brunswick to Trenton. Did you know canals were the only way livestock and farm goods were shipped in the old days, before railroads made them obsolete?" Phillip looked, but all he saw were discarded beer cans and rimless tires.

Once over the bridge, they turned right on River Road and followed the arrows into Johnson Park. PARK CLOSES AT SUNSET read the sign posted in the graveled lot.

"See that miniature racetrack?" he said, pointing to a white oval railing 50 yards to the right. "Once in a while, I see a jockey exercising a horse there. It's too small for real races. Most of the time it's empty except when they hold a fair or a flea market in the middle of it."

Phillip looked at the cinder path and pictured the center turf filled with gentlemen with colorful ascots matching their horses' silks and large suede top hats. Ladies strolled in twos,

177

twirling opened parasols and wearing high-necked dresses, while strains of "Camptown Races" filled the park. Clowns walked on stilts and jugglers flung clubs high in the air as hawkers sold beer from wooden kegs on blocks of ice.

They came to the edge of the grass. Dark-skinned children ran behind them, laughing and chasing each other. In the distance, a guitarist serenaded his girlfriend. The scent of sizzling hamburgers permeated the park from a dozen grills, and a noisy prop plane flew overhead, trailed by a yellow banner: VISIT ATLANTIC CITY.

Morris brushed some twigs off a brown slatted bench and sat down. Phillip picked up a flat stone and threw it toward the water. It sank. He looked at Morris and followed his cue to throw it sidearm. This one hit the water and jumped up, skipping two more times before sinking into the murky river.

"Phillip, I don't have to tell you what it's meant to Esther and me that you have come into our lives. After Ari died it was tough to keep going. Esther found it harder than me." Morris picked a leaf off the sole of his shoe.

Phillip sat at the edge of the bench not knowing what to say.

"After . . . she was never strong. We asked ourselves, 'Why us? What did we do wrong?'. Nothing made sense. Nothing. We waited fifteen years for Ari and then his life was snuffed out just like that." He broke a stick in half. "Why did God punish us, Phillip?"

"You didn't do anything wrong, Morris. It was an accident. God didn't punish you."

"I don't know." He rubbed his eyes. "And was it an accident you rang our doorbell?" Phillip shrugged. "Do you know what happened to the truck driver? I'll tell you," he said. "Got his license suspended for one year. Imagine that! We lost our son and he loses his driver's license for twelve months. Is that justice?"

Two more boats drifted by, and the laughing children ran near Morris and Phillip, playing tag. A corporate helicopter, from the Johnson and Johnson headquarters down river, broke the silence. Phillip got up to watch the helicopter as two football types resembling tree stumps marched in back of them. They were lugging a half-keg of beer while their girlfriends carried blankets and baskets of food. Phillip longed to be doing the same thing.

"Phillip?" Phillip was imagining himself hovering over Gillian, kissing her.

"Yes?" He was facing the river with his back to Morris.

"Esther's dying."

Phillip was still with Gillian. "I'm sorry, Morris. What'd you say?"

"Esther . . . she's dying."

"What're you talking about? She looks okay to me."

"There's no cure. She's got something called polycythemia."

"Is that when there's too many red blood cells? What's so terrible about that?" Phillip wrinkled his nose thinking she really had looked pale. He would have thought she didn't have enough red blood cells. It didn't make sense. "There must be something you can do."

"Oh, we've tried everything. When I visited you the other day, I had left her with some hotshot specialist at St. Barnabas Hospital. He was our last hope." Morris threw the broken sticks to the ground. "For years, the doctor took blood from her every few months. Drew pints and pints. 'Thinned it out,' he said. I never understood what he was doing but it worked for a long time."

"Can't they keep doing it?"

"Nah, complications. First she got phlebitis. That's why she can't stand too long."

"But President Nixon had phlebitis. He was all right."

179

"Esther's already had a minor stroke. But that's not the worst of it. It started with ringing in her ears, then pain in her joints. She'd fall back on the bed trying to get up. Those red blood cells clog every part of her body."

"Aren't there medicines for that? There's always something."

"We tried everything, even went to a faith healer. This hunchback lady filled our apartment with burning incense. The place stunk for weeks. She put her hands all over Esther's body, screamed some voodoo gibberish, rolled her eyes back, and passed out on the floor. I gave her a lot of money and when she left, Esther was the same."

"You can't give up."

"Then she almost died from too much radiation. That's when we tried chlorambucil. It controls marrow production. It worked 'til Esther got leukemia from it."

"The medicine gave her leukemia?"

"She's going to die from something—a stroke, a clot, leukemia, it's just a question of when. She was supposed to die years ago, before Ari." Morris walked to the river's edge.

"Is there anything I can do?"

"I wish there was. I just hope she doesn't suffer too much. She's in a lot of pain."

"They'll find a cure, you'll see." Morris shook his head. "Don't give up, Morris. Anything can happen."

Morris wiped his nose.

"How much time does she have?"

"Two . . . maybe three months."

❦❦

22

"**W**hat're you doing?" Trish asked as she walked past Phillip's room.

"Packing."

"Where're you going?"

Phillip didn't look at her. He flipped a handful of sweat socks into the olive-brown canvas duffle bag.

"I asked you where're you going? What's going on?"

Trish stepped into his room.

Ten cassette tapes were added to the load. "They need me. Esther's dying. Morris told me this morning."

"I'm sorry to hear that but what do you think you can do about it?"

Phillip swept his hand across his dresser, knocking over the picture of his father and brothers on a camping trip.

"Who knows how long she's got? I want to get to know her before . . . before she's gone."

He scooped a stack of tee-shirts, returned two after counting out seven, and tossed them on top of his boxer shorts.

"Look, Phillip. It's admirable you want to help but if they can't manage, there are agencies for this sort of thing."

"You're not listening to me, Mom. She's dying. I want to spend time with them."

Trish threw her hands up in the air. "You're just like your father. What's with you two? You think you're obligated to take care of the world. Believe me, you're not. Morris can take care of his wife."

"Why do you have to make this so friggin' hard? I've done everything you've ever asked. I've never given you any trouble and when I need your understanding, you tell me I'm wrong." Phillip talked so fast, spit flew from his mouth. He dropped onto his bed and cupped his face.

She stroked his hair.

"Phillip, sometimes parents understand better than children think they do. Believe me, I see what you want to do—but you're out of line. I can't let you move in with them."

"I'm eighteen and you can't stop me! And besides. . . ."

"I'm getting fed up with no one listening to me. Besides what?"

"They're my parents."

The words hung in the air long enough for both of them to hear them and hear them again. Trish stumbled back, and braced herself against the wall. Her lower lip twitched.

"I'm your mother and don't ever forget that. Your father and I raised you. We changed your diapers and held you when you cried. The Rudermans didn't do that for you. Did they bathe you with alcohol when you had the chicken pox? Did they walk you to nursery school or go to your school plays? Everything that's ever happened to you has been the result of the love and care we gave to you. So don't let me ever hear you say someone else is your parents."

"I'm sorry, I didn't mean it that way."

"If you really think they're your parents, let them pay for college."

"I know you and Dad are my parents. I don't want any others but they're not strangers to me, either. Not now. Something inside of me says I have to help."

"Phillip, what do you want me to tell you? That I want you to go? That I want you to move in with these people? Well, I can't."

"It'll only be for three weeks, then I go to Cornell. I'm not doing this to hurt you. I love you, Mom."

She wrapped her arms around him. "You know I love you, too. When will I see you again?"

"Tomorrow. I'll be here after work."

Just then, a car rumbled into the driveway.

"That's Morris. I didn't think it was right to take the Jeep."

"You can ta. . . ." He kissed her on the cheek before she finished and grabbed his bag.

Numbed and alone, Trish sat on his bed a long time.

When they got there, Morris insisted on carrying Phillip's bag. Phillip paused at the doorway. What was in store for him? As usual, pleasing smells greeted him. This time it was brisket and chicken soup. She waddled from the kitchen on her thick, rubber-soled space shoes.

"Hello." Her hands were warm, her face glowed.

Morris took him upstairs; he would stay in the extra room they had never used. It was sparsely furnished with only a mattress on a metal frame, and a night table. A frosted glass shade covered two 60-watt bulbs on the ceiling light and store-bought drapes covered the casement window.

Phillip placed his clothes on the empty shelves and on hangers in the closet, ignoring a cardboard box on the floor. It was like living in a hotel.

Esther moved about with an all-but-forgotten energy. She had straightened the house that afternoon, humming all the while. Hearing Phillip in his room, she sat Morris down.

"It's wrong. You shouldn't have let him come, Moishe."

"I couldn't stop him. He's got your stubborn streak. It'll only be for a few days and then you'll see, he'll return home. Besides, he *is* our son."

She put her face to his and whispered in hissing tones.

"Don't ever say that again. We buried our son, may he rest in peace, and don't ever forget that, Morris Ruderman."

"Calm down, Essie. I got to thinking how Phillip's got our blood in him. It's gotta count for something."

"Only in tests I don't understand. He's a nice boy. The Hunters did a good job with him, but a son to us? Never." She pounded her brittle chest. "Heart is what it's all about, and Ari had ours." Without another word, Esther glided to the stove and skimmed off gobbets of fat floating on top of the chicken soup.

New footsteps approached.

"Is there anything you need?" Esther asked, wiping her hands in her apron.

"I've got everything, thank you."

"Do you want a cold drink?"

"Yes, please." She poured lemonade, which was his favorite drink. Gone in one swallow, her face lit up when he asked for more.

"Sit, sit." Morris tapped the kitchen chair and the three of them looked at each other. They nodded, smiled, sighed, and cleared their throats.

"How are you feeling?" Phillip asked Esther.

"Some days I don't feel so good. Today," she smiled, "today, I feel better."

Morris stood.

"I'll be back in a few minutes, Phillip." He waved a piece of paper in the air. "One of the hazards of marriage: lists. There's always something the missus wants. Be right back."

Phillip sipped a second glass of lemonade while Esther fussed at the stove. She asked questions about his brothers and parents and giggled when he talked about Gillian.

"Why do you want to be a vet, Phillip? I didn't see any pets in your home."

His mind drifted to the night before.

He blessed Mrs. Davis for seeing Miss Saigon. *Making love was better the second time . . . Gilly said it didn't hurt. He had been able to control himself, at least for a while, before exploding.*

The wallpaper in Esther's kitchen was faded. The once bright red roses tattooed to the pink and beige background were now wilted. Above his head, he heard the hum of the transformer under the tarnished canopy. One 32-watt fluorescent bulb lit the kitchen.

Eventually, Trish got off Phillip's bed. She picked up the trophy his Little League team had won and was surprised at how light it was. She thumbed through a magazine on his desk. She looked at the remaining CDs arranged alphabetically in their black plastic rack. She opened one of his drawers and smelled his shirts, which had his scent. She let her fingers touch the lips of his graduation picture.

Trish went downstairs to the den and filled a glass with scotch. She sipped some to make room for the ice cubes. The liquor brought back memories of her childhood. She smelled her father's breath . . . then her mother's—smells of fear, of nights of terror while lying still . . . afraid to sleep.

She stared blindly, drinking and smoking.

"Hey, what's this?" Brad had returned from playing golf with Rick Sturnweiss. Trish remained motionless, her legs crossed. He walked toward her.

"Sit down," she ordered.

He complied.

"Isn't it a bit early for a drink?"

She spoke with a glazed face.

"Phillip moved in with the Rudermans."

"Why, for heaven's sake? Didn't you try to stop him?"

"Seems he thinks he's old enough to do what he wants." Trish told him about Esther's illness and how Phillip was determined to live with them.

"Phillip's doing what we raised him to do, be responsible, helpful to others. Frankly, I'm proud of him."

"Leave it to you to find good out of this! Our family's crumbling and you think he did the right thing. Susan was right: men are screwed up. They don't know anything about people or feelings. All they know is this macho shit of control, of leading the tribe."

"What are you talking about?"

"Let me put it to you this way. God is a man! How else could you explain the stupid things men do? A female God would never let anyone be so fucked up."

"You're drunk. I don't blame you for being upset, but this is not a big deal."

She lit another cigarette and finished her drink. Her lips were drawn tight while she considered what to say.

"Brad, you're an ass. I don't know when it happened, or how I missed it, but you are not the emotionally responsible man I married. Phillip will be okay, that much I'm sure of. But I don't know what happened to us, where we stopped discussing things, when you went off on a tangent. All I know is that you've damaged me."

186

Brad poured himself a scotch and finished it in one swallow.

"I messed up, didn't I?"

"You did what you had to do."

23

❧❧

"**H**ow's it going?" Steve Sadler asked. His blue shirt made his hazel eyes azure.

"You won't believe the latest, Phillip's moved in with the Rudermans."

"Is she a better cook?"

"Oh shit. You, too? I thought you'd be more understanding."

"I am, Trish, that's what we call *humor.*"

"Sorry, but I seem to have lost mine. Yesterday, Morris, he's Phillip's biological father, told him Esther has terminal leukemia or something like it. Without consulting us, Phillip moved in with them."

"That's kind of noble, but I don't see anything wrong with that. He's just a kid doing what he thinks is right. Give him space, Trish. He'll be back."

"How can you be so sure?" She grabbed his arm.

Steve leaned forward and electricity arced between their bodies. She tipped her head and brushed the hair from her face. Her hand remained on his arm. She slid her fingers down to meet his and the touch of their fingertips made her wet. He kneeled and was at eye level with her, and she forgot about Phillip for the first time in weeks.

"Steve, I can't . . . I don't. . . ."

Their heads almost touched.

"Trust me. Everything will work out. I promise you, everything."

Later, Phillip walked through the door on Coddington Terrace.

"How was your first night at the Rudermans'?" Trish asked.

"It was okay, Mom."

"And work?"

"Frank thinks we're due for a major breakthr. . . ."

"Tell me about last night. How were they?"

"Fine."

"Only fine?"

"They couldn't have been nicer. But it's not the same as here. I miss you guys," Phillip said and hugged her.

"I may not approve of what you're doing, but I'm proud of you. Don't forget, your room's always waiting for you."

"I know, but I've got to stick it out a while longer."

"I know."

Esther grabbed the vinyl-covered kitchen chair for support; the pain was getting worse. Phillip sprung to his feet and helped her ease onto the seat.

"Get me my pills, Phillip," she wheezed. Fumbling with the plastic safety cap on the iodine-yellow vial, he coaxed a lemon colored Percodan into his palm.

"Here."

He watched her throw her head back, taking it without water.

"I'll be okay, Phillip."

"I'm going to unload the dishwasher."

"That won't be. . . ."

"Shhhh, Esther, I know how to put dishes away. You take it easy."

"I do feel a little tired, Phillip. I think I'll lie down for a minute."

Each day a similar scene unfolded: Esther tried to perform a once normal task but felt fatigued, pain became her constant companion. The narcotic made her sleepy and she spent more time in bed.

While she slept, Morris regaled Phillip with stories of ancient Newark. He told Phillip it had its own orchestra and he had heard great philharmonics from all over the world at the Mosque Theater, the city's version of Carnegie Hall. He and Esther frequented the Yiddish Theater until no one went anymore. On Sundays they would go to Weequahic Park and have picnics where the Leni-Lenape Indians once stalked. Afterward, they would row in the catfish-filled lake across from the Tavern Restaurant that, in its day, was comparable to The Palm or Peter Luger's in New York.

It had been a wonderful city until the riots, more than two decades earlier, caused the city's vital signs to flutter. Newark became the first American city placed on a respirator, mired in an urban intensive care. But the city's pulse lingered. "Where there's life, there's always hope," Morris said. And when he was talked out, they went to sleep.

The same pattern followed the next day, then the next.

Friday Phillip arrived from work in time to see Morris wrestle with the living room sofa.

"Thank God you're here. Grab the other end," Morris said to Phillip as he entered the living room. Phillip positioned himself and on the count of three, they lifted the heavy sofa. Morris backpedaled to the space the dining room table once occupied, which was now against the wall.

"What's next?"

"That's it." Morris looked at his watch. "The hospital bed's supposed to be delivered any minute. Esther finally gave in. She can't climb the stairs anymore."

"I'm going to get something," Phillip said.

Taking the steps three at a time, Phillip got the television he had brought from his house and set it on the coffee table where Esther could watch her favorite shows.

The doorbell rang. Two scrawny, olive-skinned Spanish-speaking men with wisps of goatees struggled with the bed. A stream of curses flew from their mouths. It looked too wide to get through the door. They were arguing with each other when Phillip intervened.

"Stand the bed on its end. You can wiggle it through."

Once they left, Phillip and Morris rearranged the furniture until they were satisfied it was to Esther's liking. Phillip fetched a glass of water.

"Go to bed, Phillip. Your eyes look glazed."

"I am tired. G'night, Morris."

The room was hot and stuffy, and he tossed and turned. Eventually, he fell into a restless sleep. In what seemed like moments, chirping sparrows greeted him. The sun had not yet made its way through the rusted metal window, but instinct told him it would be another stifling day. The sheets were damp with perspiration and the comforter was on the floor. There was a wet spot were saliva had dripped from his mouth.

He pulled cut-off jeans over his shorts, whose white border inched below the frayed denim, and trod to the pink-tiled guest bathroom. With the light still off, he splashed water on his face. Morris's door was open; the room empty. Enticed by the smell of brewed coffee, Phillip trekked down the thinly carpeted stairs. His bare foot touched the landing when he saw Esther propped in her new bed, gazing out the bay window.

"Good morning, Phillip," she said without turning.

"Good morning, Esther. How'd you sleep?" She was sipping tea. Dry toast with jam was untouched on the tray to her side.

"Not that well. The noises from the street kept me up most of the night."

Morris entered wearing black gabardine pants and an open-collared powder blue shirt with the insignia of a turtle over the breast pocket.

"Breakfast?"

"French toast . . . your way," Phillip answered.

Phillip watched Morris crack the eggs with one hand, add milk, salt and pepper, before scrambling them. He let the sliced bread soak until it was saturated. Browned to perfection, Morris sprinkled cinnamon on top.

"Great, Morris. They're really great. My father makes great pancakes."

"I bet he does. Fathers and cooking breakfast go hand-in-hand, don't they?"

"They sure do."

By the time Phillip finished his second serving, Esther was dozing. Phillip cleared the table and washed the dishes while Morris went to the market. Phillip gingerly removed the tray next to Esther.

"Phillip?" He stopped in his tracks.

"I didn't mean to wake you."

"I was up. Sit with me."

"I was going to my room."

"Sit with me."

She smoothed the blanket.

He looked down; her body had shriveled in a week's time, like a tire going flat. Skin hung from her; air hissed as she struggled to breathe. He was half-sitting, half-standing by the edge of the bed.

192

"Phillip?" She moved her bony leg.

"Esther? Es. . . ." Her eyelids no longer fluttered. This time she slept. Phillip returned to his room to wait for Morris. He pried open a book, but didn't feel like reading. Then he remembered the box.

He opened the closet door and pulled it over the door sill and lifted the intercrossed flaps that had been closed for the last four years. A layer of dust flew in his face. He sneezed. Phillip took inventory of its contents.

Gently, he lifted a blue plastic covered album and opened it. Pressed under the cover was a clipping from the *Jewish News* that heralded a baby boy born to Esther and Morris Ruderman of Newark, New Jersey. There were pictures of Ari wrapped in a blanket, Ari lying on a blanket, Ari crying, looking at a mobile, standing in his crib, in a walker and crawling. His parents had the same poses of him.

Page after page revealed a happy child, a loved child. Phillip smiled at a slimmer Morris with lots of dark hair and a younger, healthier, and taller-looking Esther. There were pictures at the beach, on swings, in the water. There were photos of Ari with one friend in particular. Phillip slid one picture from the sleeve. "Ari and Randy, July, 1985." The two boys appeared in many others.

He rummaged through the rest. There were certificates for perfect attendance at grammar school, Presidential physical fitness awards, report cards and loose pictures, a baseball hat—he loved the Mets, too!—and a Swiss Army knife with more blades than his. Phillip picked up the bronzed baby shoes and pictured a little boy taking his first steps.

He shuddered at the sight of an autographed Tom Seaver mitt. It was well-worn. He slipped his hand inside and turned it over. They both kept their index fingers on the outside. Leaving it on, Phillip pulled his knees to his chest, clasping his legs tightly.

"It's stiff," he said out loud, "I'll oil it for you."

He rocked back and forth.

"Damn it, Ari, why'd you have to die?"

24

❧❧

"It's been ages! I wondered when I'd ever see you again." Myrna kissed Trish on both cheeks before following the waitress to a table.

"Thank God for weekends. This is the first time I've had a minute to myself. Brad's playing golf and Ron and Todd are off somewhere." Myrna ordered a fruit salad platter and Trish ordered a cheeseburger and fries.

"Sorry. I'll blow the smoke in the other direction," Trish said, lighting a cigarette.

"I really thought you were avoiding me," Myrna said.

"How could you think that? I never blamed Frank. I admit he wasn't my favorite person when this started. I wish he had listened when you tried to talk him out of telling us in the first place."

"It would've made things a lot easier. How're you and Brad holding up?"

"Funny you should ask," Trish said.

"What do you mean?"

"Well, Brad would say our marriage is in choppy waters but the seas will calm. The guy's an eternal optimist."

"Sweetie, Brad's terrific and you know it."

"It's been so hard dealing with this nightmare."

"Of course it's a nightmare; finding out that Phillip wasn't yours—it would shock anyone," Myrna said.

"That's not what I'm upset about. It's Brad."

Myrna twisted her mouth and arched her eyebrows. Trish continued.

"What's got me is Brad ruining my family like Daddy did."

"Daddy didn't ruin our family."

"Myrna?"

"Yes?"

"Did Daddy . . . ?"

"Did Daddy what?"

"Did he ever touch you?" Trish asked.

"Of course he touched me. We always held hands when we walked . . . and . . . and he held me a lot when we went swimming. He was always kissing me."

"How did he kiss you, Myrna?"

"Like any father would kiss a daughter."

"We only had *this* father. How did he kiss you? On the lips?"

"Of course! Where else would he kiss me when I was little?"

"And when you got older? Where?"

"Always on the lips. What're you getting at, Trish?"

"Did he . . . ever. . . ."

Myrna leaned forward, her lips blanching.

"Oh boy!" Trish said, noting water marks on the acoustic tiles. "This is harder than I thought."

"What are you getting at?"

"Okay. I will. Did he ever fondle you or . . . or have sex with you?" Trish exhaled the words and grimaced at the horrible images rattling in her head.

"Oh, that! Sure, he fondled me. Something about not playing football 'cause I was a girl. We made a game of it. Mommy told me every father did those things to their daughters."

"Myrna! What's wrong with you? How could you think that was normal? Daddy took advantage of us, and Mommy let him. Otherwise, he'd beat her."

"I loved Daddy."

"So did I . . . but he hurt us, Myrna."

"I know." Myrna's hands fell onto her lap.

"What did you say? I couldn't hear you?"

"I said, I know he hurt us. I could never admit it . . . I felt sorry for him when he lost his job."

"But you were already in college. He took it out on me. Why didn't you say something to me? Warn me?"

"You were little. I thought he'd leave you alone. Besides, I wasn't sure what normal was. He really wasn't bad with me." Myrna snapped her head back. "But I love Frank. He's the best thing that ever happened to me, just like Brad is for you. Brad loves you, Trish. You have to see that. Once Brad found out, he had to tell Phillip. That's the way he is."

"But he didn't have to help him," Trish fished for a Kleenex in her purse.

"In Brad's mind he did. Stop fighting him. Everything will work out. You'll see."

"I hope so. I'm sick about Phillip moving out."

Trish looked through reddened eyes. She blew her nose and unscrewed her lipstick case. "I nearly did something very foolish." She blotted the excess on the napkin. "I hope it's not too late."

"Trish, it's never too late to do the right thing."

That night, Trish dropped Ron and Todd at the Colony Theater. When she returned, she found Brad leafing through *Forbes* magazine in the den.

197

"Can we talk? There's something you need to hear. It's about my father."

Brad closed the magazine. "I'm listening."

"I've never told this to anyone. Myrna and I met for lunch today . . . it happened to her, too, well, not as bad."

"Uh, could you be a little more specific?"

Trish wiggled and scratched and longed for a confessional booth, so she wouldn't have to face Brad.

"Do you remember me telling you how my mother could never accept the fact that we weren't as well-off as our relatives? She berated my father every chance she could. It got to be too much for him. He started drinking. Most of the time, he passed out on the kitchen table or in front of the television.

"In the summer, when my mother wore sleeveless dresses, there'd be black and blue marks on her arms. I asked her where she got them but she pretended not to hear me. When his drinking got bad, she locked him out of their bedroom. That's when he crawled into my bed."

Tears rolled down her face.

"Christ! I never had a clue."

She continued. "Myrna was in high school then. He told me he did it with her, too, but I had always been too afraid to ask. For a year or so, nothing much happened. I hated his drunken breath, I never got used to it. Then Myrna went to college, and things changed.

"Dad hit his foreman after the man filed a complaint about Dad's performance. Dad was getting to work late every day and making lots of mistakes. Then he was around the house all the time and Mom started drinking. He used to beat her up, but she never complained.

"One day, she came into my room and told me to be nice to Daddy. 'Do whatever he wants,' she said. I didn't know what she meant at the time, but I loved my parents.

So I listened. That's when he stopped beating her. In some warped way, my father was happy for the first time in his life."

By now, Trish was sobbing.

"And do you know what made him happy?" she said in a cold voice.

"Trish, you don't have to tell me anymore." Brad put his arm around her.

"I have to. I've kept this inside me nearly thirty years. There were times I thought I'd lose my mind."

"It must've been a nightmare." He stroked her hair.

"I hated him, Brad. He would touch me all over. At first he was gentle. But the drunker he got, the rougher he liked it. He came to me almost every night. What did I know? I thought I was being a good girl. He never hit me, not like he did to her. I was afraid to tell anyone. Not even Myrna."

She wiped her eyes.

"College was out of the question. We had no money but that didn't matter: I had to get away. But I kept picking the wrong men until I met you. You were too good to be true, Brad. You were kind and gentle, you made me happy. That's why I can't accept this thing with Phillip. It spoiled my dreams."

"Honey, do you think I did any of this to hurt you? Shit, I can't believe what you went through. Everything's going to be all right, I just know it. Listen, if you want to get professional help, I'm all for it. We can go together."

"I can't think of that right now, Brad. It means a lot to me that you offered, and maybe we'll go one day. But telling you and dealing with it is such a relief. You've been rock solid for everything, even about Phillip, and I love you for it. I just wish you weren't so goddamned honest about telling him. It would've saved us a lot of grief."

"Maybe it's the best thing that ever happened to us. Who knows?"

She stood and flicked the light switch off.

"What gives? What're you doing?"

"I got an sudden urge."

"Just like that?" he asked.

"Yup, just like that," she answered, pulling him onto the beige, white, and brown throw rug. There was no further debate; she helped him undress. Their lips met.

"Put this pillow under your head."

Brad leaned back and extended his arms as if doing a back float, while circuits of energy pulsed from his beacon. His instrument grew in her mouth every time she went down, like a slide trombone reaching for new notes. He arched as her lips tripped over the ultra-sensitive rim, he gasped each time she trapped the delicate skin between her teeth. She nibbled and licked and altered the tempo. She toyed with him until Brad writhed in libidinal syncopation. Ready to burst, she swallowed its total length, driving him to that twilight zone where differences between pain and pleasure become hazy, at best. His body was off the floor by now.

He screamed, then collapsed.

She continued to lick him, like a kitten cleaning its paw. His racing chest slowed and his breathing finally returned to normal. He stirred.

"That was unbelievable. What did I do to deserve this?"

"Let's just say it's for being you," she said, reaching for a tissue. "And if you're good, I'll. . . ."

"You'll what?" he asked.

"Do it again."

25

❧❧

Sunday morning Phillip picked Gillian up to go to Livingston's municipal pool. When she heard the honk, she yelled to her mother, slammed the door, and loped across her lawn with a towel dangling from her beach bag.

"How's Esther?"

"She's brave. Tries to act normal but her face gets all twisted. The pain's real bad. It's killing Morris."

"That's awful. She seems so nice."

"Yeah, I like her."

"Did you miss me?" she asked.

A smile crept across Phillip's face. "I couldn't wait to see you. Having two sets of parents takes a lot of time."

He parked the car. They held hands in spite of carrying a blanket, two small chairs, towels, a radio, and a beach bag. Everyday "regulars" staked claim to the shady areas; they guarded these protected patches like sentries on night watch—no intruders were allowed in their zones. Gillian and Phillip spread their blanket in an open, sunny area— next to the kiddie pool.

"Here," she said, and shoved a paper in front of his face. "It's for you. Read it."

Gillian covered her mouth and followed his eyes as they moved from line to line. She blinked when he blinked, moved her lips with his.

a small boy with bushy hair and sea-green eyes
pranced upon virgin white sands
in search of his goal—
to find the perfect seashell

day after day, he roamed the beaches
until he grew weary, losing hope
then a wave broke before him
uncovering a huge rainbow-colored shell
bathed in the tears of millennia long past

he labored to put the shell to the final test
to hear its mighty roar
but nothing was forthcoming
sadness overcame him as he threw it down
shattering it in the silica of time
into the rocks of ages long gone

just then, a dancing trinket floated to his feet
grasping it with tiny fingers
he cocked his arm to hurl it
when it sang a sweet gentle melody to him
he laughed a deep laugh from his soul
as the shell told him of the wonders of the
ancients. . . . of wisdom and time
of the secrets of the sand
and of himself.

"Gilly! This is incredible!" He threw the poem down and pulled her toward him.

"Do you like it? Do you really like it?" She closed her eyes, waiting for the truth.

"Like it? I love it! You're the best." They spent the rest of the day intertwined as if they were the only ones at the pool.

"What time is it?" Phillip asked when he realized the crowd had thinned.

"Nearly dinner time," she answered.

"Shit!" Phillip sprung to his feet. "I promised Morris that I'd meet him at seven-thirty. He's got something he wants to do or show me. I didn't quite get what it was."

Gillian pouted. "I never get to see you anymore."

"Sorry, babe, I got to do this."

Phillip followed Morris's directions and exited Route 18 at George Street. Ancient oak and crusty birch trees lined the street that cut Rutgers' sister college, Douglass, in half. Turning onto Joyce Kilmer Avenue, he wondered if these were the trees that had inspired New Brunswick's famous poet to pen: "I think that I shall never see/A poem as lovely as a tree."

Phillip found Greene Street. Rubble greeted his gaze. Number 1460 was the lone standing building amidst a field of broken bricks and strewn beer bottles. Signs of urban reconstruction abounded in the city but this block served as a reminder of New Brunswick's decayed past.

Silhouetted by modern structures and the Frog and the Peach Restaurant on the next block, Phillip wondered why Morris wanted to meet him there. Under the pointed roof was a blue and green stained glass window laced with flashes of red and orange. Below it a white sign with black lettering: CONGREGATION BETH SHALOM

Phillip mounted the cracked limestone steps, holding onto the black rail that bisected the length of the building. He tugged the wrought-iron handle. It was locked. He tried the other entry and it swung open noiselessly.

Inside, the heavy door closed and canceled the intrusive

light that invaded the darkened sanctuary. He waited for his eyes to adjust to the dim light.

"Hello?" Phillip said, in a barely audible voice. A door clicked and he jumped. "Morris, is that you?"

"Phillip? Hope I didn't scare you."

"Nope."

"Good. Come this way." Morris led him down a flight of well-polished marble stairs that were worn in the center by countless worshippers using the facility for a hundred years. Phillip hugged the wall until they reached the bottom where he found himself in a square room with four rows of wooden benches facing a small pulpit. A lantern, a small red light, which remained lit at all times, burned above the ark holding the sacred prayer scrolls.

"Phillip, I'm glad you came; Esther was too weak. It's a special day."

"What is it?"

"Ari died four years ago today. They were smart!"

"Who was?"

"Whoever thought up these Jewish customs, that's who. When a family member dies, Jews mourn for one year in a group of people. They call it a *minyan*. Grieving in public forces you to deal with death so you can get on with your life. Otherwise, those feelings stay bottled up inside. Esther refuses to come here. She says there can be no God if children can be killed."

"But that's not true, Morris. Accidents happen. God can't be expected to watch over everyone," Phillip said.

Noises distracted them. A hearty band of men in their fifties and sixties filed into the small room. They took their accustomed places and began praying in rapid-fire Hebrew.

Phillip watched in fascination. They mumbled and sang in no particular fashion. Some weaved from left to right and some bobbed back and forth. Random "Amens" were emit-

204

ted whenever they wanted, or so it seemed.

The mourner's prayer, called the Kaddish, was chanted in unison. Each man paid homage to a departed family member and, in spite of their loss, Morris explained later, they prayed for the love and glorification of their Lord. The murmuring stopped. They shook hands and left twelve minutes later.

Esther was waiting for them. After a dinner of tuna fish on a bagel and a garden salad, Phillip excused himself and went to his room. Morris remained downstairs and talked until her drugs took effect. Satisfied she was asleep for the night, he mounted the stairs. He lay down on his side of the bed and slept in his clothes.

The next evening Phillip waited on South Livingston Avenue, beyond Northfield Center, for a clearing in the traffic. He made a sharp left into the unpaved parking lot, skidding on the blue-gray stones. When he reached the sidewalk, he saw Trish in front of Sam's Clothing Store. A crushed cigarette was under her shoe.

"Hi! Did you call ahead?" he asked.

"Jeff said he'd have the clothes laid out for you. He knows how much you adore shopping. Phillip, are you eating enough? You look too thin."

"Mom, I weigh the same. You forgot what I look like."

Phillip's idea of collegiate garb consisted of tee shirts, sweat shirts, and jeans. Trish wanted gabardine slacks, collared shirts, and at least one sports jacket. Compromises made, they finished two hours later.

"That wasn't too bad, was it, Phillip?"

"No. Neither's having your wisdom teeth pulled!"

"How about ice cream at Don's?" she asked.

"Sounds good to me. Race you."

"Drive carefully."

A sun-bleached blond with a turned up nose named Haley waited on them.

"I'd like a chocolate ice cream soda with coffee ice cream, please," Phillip said.

"Black coffee for me."

Phillip followed her tanned legs.

"Not as cute as Gillian," Trish said.

"I know, just looking. Mom? I need to talk to you about college."

"I hope you didn't take me seriously; you know we're still paying for it. Phillip, you are going, aren't you? I don't think I could take another surprise."

"Of course I'm going."

"Then what is it, Phillip?" He looked at her, wide-eyed.

"I don't want to go to Cornell anymore."

"Why not? You were so excited to get in there. It was your first choice! You do want to be a vet, don't you?"

"Ummm . . . not exactly."

"Did Morris put you up to this?"

"No! Honest, he didn't. He doesn't know about this."

"Okay, I'm listening." She leaned back and folded her arms.

"I did want to go Cornell. The school's so beautiful and it has the best vet program in the East."

"Soooo?"

"I don't want to be a vet anymore. I want to do research . . . like Uncle Frank does."

"Look where his research has gotten us."

"C'mon, Mom. Frank's a great researcher, but he's not the issue. This summer, I loved setting up the experiments, using the microscopes, making the slides. It was neat trying to solve the research problems—every day was a new dilemma. And I'd still be working with animals."

"But it's too late to change schools. Where would you go?"

"Rutgers."

"Rutgers? Why there?"

"Cook College. It's their agricultural school. They have a program in animal physiology. Some of the classes are even in the medical school."

"Can you get in? School starts in a couple of weeks."

His white teeth sparkled against his tan skin.

"I'm already in! All I need is your approval . . . and Dad's."

"God, when you make up your mind, there's no stopping you, is there?"

"Not really."

"So now you'll be closer to Gillian and the Rudermans, how cozy."

"Don't forget I'll be closer to you, too. What do you say? Can I go to Rutgers?"

"What's there to say? Good luck, Phillip."

"Mom, you're the greatest!"

26

❦❦

There was one week left in August. Phillip and Gillian celebrated their last Saturday down the shore drinking beer, vodka, and tequila slammers. He would never do it again. Gillian must have driven him home. His parched mouth felt filled with sand, his head ached, and his eyelids were nailed shut.

Street noises barged through the open window. Phillip prayed they would go away. He turned over and peeked from under the covers anticipating blinding light. He was right. It was too bright so he retreated under the comforter to the soft, welcome darkness. That only worked for a little while. Motivated by a growling stomach, Phillip mustered his courage to venture into the cosmic abyss of a sunny Sunday morning in the Ruderman household.

Shuffling to what had become his bathroom, Phillip washed his face and brushed the furry film off his teeth. Visceral senses returned like novocaine wearing off. He approached the steps timidly, clutching the rail to halt the swaying apartment. At the bottom, he saw her head turned its usual direction toward the window.

"Is that you, Phillip?"

"Yes, Esther."

"Where's Morris?"

"Taking a shower."

She waved her hand like a traffic cop, directing him closer. "Sit by me, Phillip." Her eyes were clear and steady. There was color, long missing, in her cheeks.

"Can I get you anything, Esther? You look better today."

"Not now, Phillip. I want to tell you about my dream."

"Sure, tell me about your dream," he said, and took her outstretched hand. There was no flesh left, just bones. Her blind gaze passed through him.

"Last night I was cold, very cold. I thought I was delirious from the pain medication but it had worn off a long time before. You know I hate taking those pills."

"I know."

"Just as I fell asleep, he appeared!" There was a fiery spark in her eyes.

"Who was there, Esther? Who?"

"Why, Ari, of course!"

"Ari? What do you mean, Esther?"

"It was Ari, I tell you. He was here, in my dream. At first, I thought he was alive. He looked so real. I tried to touch him. But then I remembered it was a dream and I couldn't hold him like I wanted to."

"Did he say anything?"

"Not at first. He floated . . . like a balloon, waving back and forth in a gentle breeze. And then . . . he talked."

"What'd he say?"

"Phillip, he said he watches me all the time. Can you believe that?" She lifted her emaciated arm and pointed with a skeleton's finger toward the ceiling. "There, he watched from there . . . in the corner. And you know what else?" He shook his head. "He had on the same faded jeans and the shirt with a picture of the Doors on it. He didn't grow at all!" she said, shaking her head. "It's been four years, you know."

209

"I know, Esther." Phillip wasn't sure if she was hallucinating or dreaming but what was the difference? A hacking cough shook her. When the pain passed, she gathered her energy.

"Oh, Phillip," she said happily, "you should've seen his smile. His teeth were so white. We talked about his friends, the ones he used to play with when we lived in our house." She turned with a bashful grin. "I told him about you. Yes, I did. I told him you were a wonderful young man, and that you came from a nice family. He said he saw you in the room upstairs."

"What else did he say?" Her wasted face struggled to recall every detail.

"Talking with him made the coldness go away. I became warm. Then, a miracle happened . . . the pain, it went away. The more we talked, the more the pain disappeared. Oh, Phillip, he was better than all the medicines and all the doctors in the whole world."

"I'm sure he was."

"And you know what else?"

"What, Esther?"

"He tried to touch me! Our fingers almost touched. He said, 'Soon, soon, I'll see you soon.' What do you suppose he meant, Phillip?"

"I don't know. Maybe he'll visit tomorrow. You said he's been here before."

"He has, he told me so."

"Well, I don't know *what* you saw but you look better this morning." She coughed again and asked for water.

Phillip put the glass on the table, and searched for the button to raise the back of the bed. Esther motioned when she was comfortable. As he had learned to do from the visiting nurse, he eased an open palm under her shoulder blade and nudged her feeble body to him.

Her eyes were filled with joyful clarity—she had communed with her dead son and made her peace. Phillip held the glass as she lowered her head, her cracked blue lips twitched. Like a cawing crow, she shrieked. Her head snapped to the side. There was a gurgle from the back of her throat, a ghostly ripple then no more. Her bloated tongue blocked her air passage and her eyes rolled under her top lids, no longer responsive to the room's ghastly light.

He didn't know what to do. The hand supporting her shook, her body vibrated, her head bobbed from side to side.

"Morris! Morris! Help!"

Phillip screamed again but nothing came out; air was needed to pass over the vocal cords . . . and Phillip Hunter had none. He held death in his arms, it smiled back serenely; he screamed in silent terror.

By this time, Morris had reached the bottom of the stairs. He took Phillip's arm and eased Esther onto the bed. He guided Phillip backward, and together, they sat in a chair. Morris stroked Phillip's back, cradling his head to his breast. Morris said nothing. There was nothing to say. The two men rocked in the chair for an eternity, and all the while, Esther slept.

Feeling the boy's body relax against his, Morris pushed himself up, still keeping a hand on Phillip's shoulder. Phillip wiped his face in his shirt.

Bent and tired, Morris looked at her. He knew she was with Ari. He pulled aside the blanket; there was so little of her left. He put an elbow down, then pulled his leg over the side. Morris Ruderman kissed her . . . then kissed her again, nestling next to his once beautiful bride.

27

꙳꙳

A billboard with changeable letters directed Phillip to the Ruderman funeral. He saw Morris talking with animated gestures to a man with a book under his arm.

"Uhhumm. Uhhumm." Phillip cleared his throat.

"Oh, Phillip, you're here. Let me introduce you to my Rabbi. Rabbi Jacobowitz, this is Phillip, Phillip Hunter."

The short man's threadbare funeral suit was partially covered by a flowing steel-colored beard. He adjusted the brim of his black felt hat, shifted the prayer book to his left hand, and greeted Phillip.

"Morris tells me you were Ari's friend."

"Uh, yes, I was. It's a pleasure to meet you."

"Next time, under better circumstances," the rabbi said.

"Excuse us, Rabbi." Morris pulled Phillip's arm. "Come, I want you to see the casket before the others arrive." Phillip swallowed hard, trailing Morris by a step. Fortunately, the casket was closed.

"Who's that?" Phillip whispered. They were in the sanctuary of the funeral parlor. The room was all wood, stained blond and highly lacquered. A thick maroon carpet served as a runway across the front and center aisles. The plush bench cushions were the same color. Phillip looked up and noticed the vaulted ceiling. The length and breadth of the dome-like ceiling, and the absence of windows, made the room feel as though it were a coffin itself. The room's air was rarified, as he imagined it would be at high altitudes; there was barely enough to breathe.

A man sat in a chair next to Esther's head, holding an open book. He bobbed from the waist, often wailing a word or two, oblivious to their presence.

"He's a member of the synagogue. When someone dies, a representative of the congregation stays with the body for the entire night . . . so it won't be alone. This man does it for a living."

They returned to the anteroom where Morris received the few remaining friends that would come. Phillip stayed by his side and, if someone asked, he was an old friend of Ari's. Most people mumbled a few inaudible words and quickly moved on.

Men in black suits wearing dark sunglasses ushered the guests into the sanctuary. Morris and Phillip stayed behind. The doors were closing when a lanky boy, an inch or two taller than Phillip, rushed toward them. The youth was too thin for his clothes and wore a diamond stud in his left ear.

"Randy? Is that you?"

"Mr. Ruderman, I'm glad I got here in time," the gawky teenager said. Phillip recognized him as the boy in all the photographs.

"It's been four years! Look how you've grown!" Morris pulled him closer. "Phillip, I want you to meet Ari's best friend, Randy Bressman." They shook hands. "Phillip is . . . a new friend."

The usher herded Randy inside like a stray calf, then returned and asked Morris and Phillip to follow. A hush overcame the mourners.

The rabbi began. Morris asked him to make the service brief and he did. Having heard the few eloquent words, everyone followed the hearse to the cemetery located off Exit 135 of the Garden State Parkway.

There was little traffic on the way. The small caravan, each with its headlights on to let the world know they were communing with the dead, pulled into the Mt. Zion Cemetery. It was barren of visitors.

Nervous chatter filled the time until the funeral director gathered the pallbearers. Without fanfare, they slid the pine casket from the hearse onto a reinforced stretcher and rolled it toward the freshly dug grave.

Brad and Trish pulled behind the last car as the graveside service began. They stood in back. The sun beat down on the mournful gathering. The air was humid and thick. Sweat trickled down Brad's back. He swatted at a bee next to Trish's head.

The rabbi chanted with eyes shut; the book remained closed in his palm. Ritualistic prayers asked for eternal peace and rest for Esther. Phillip put his arm around Morris as the casket was suspended over the grave on thick metal bars connected to an electric crank that lowered it into the ground. Once the coffin disappeared, the straps supporting it were pulled out by the grave diggers.

Rabbi Jacobowitz took a shovel and stuck it in the fresh earth and threw it onto the casket. It landed with a dull thud, pebbles rolling across the top. He handed the shovel to Morris who repeated the action with a slight hesitation. Hearing the noise made Morris stronger, and he threw more dirt. He did it one more time before it was Phillip's turn.

Phillip panicked. He had never seen a coffin let alone thrown dirt on one. Morris nudged him, but he just stood there. Morris nudged him again and Phillip did it. One by one, those who wanted to throw dirt threw it until the fresh wood was covered, creating a brown mound that rose to a peak.

Trish looked about the cemetery. Tufts of grass in hard-to-reach places detracted from the clipped grounds. Olive-sized rocks were left on headstones, remembrances by visitors earlier in the week. Trish yawned as Brad stepped forward to take the shovel. The crowd had thinned and only four people remained.

The rabbi moved to take the wooden handle from Brad and that's when she saw it! She staggered, nearly losing her balance, prompting Brad to bolt forward to help her. With her right hand extended like a divining rod, Trish was drawn to a gray and white flecked granite tombstone with the Star of David at its top. The inscription was etched boldly:

Ari Kenneth Ruderman
March 21, 1975 - August 22, 1989
Beloved Son Who Died
In the Springtime of His Life

"Brad! That's him!" He stumbled, too, but regained his balance. Trish buried her face in his jacket. They were standing in front of the grave of a son both had held eighteen years ago.

Brad remembered the boy's screams, his scarlet cheeks, and tiny fingers. He only stopped crying when the nurse gave him to his mother. Trish held him to her breast, oblivious to the doctor sewing her up. She looked beautiful then, and so very happy.

Now it was the mother's turn to scream. Trish lifted her head and looked over his shoulder. On shaky legs, she stood at the tombstone, mouthing the words of the inscription over and over. She dropped to her knees, leaned over, and kissed the smooth stone.

28

❦❦

It had been less than ten weeks since the strains of "Pomp and Circumstance" filled his ears, less than ten weeks since he learned about genetically bred mice. And now, Phillip Hunter found himself spending the last days of August mourning a mother he had only recently come to know. He and Morris received the few visitors who came to pay their respects. Some found it easier to send flowers or a basket of fruit rather than face the survivors.

Phillip didn't spend every minute mourning; Morris encouraged him to get ready for college. Fortunately, he received a room assignment when a student cancelled at the last minute. He would be living in the "Quad," a series of aged buildings on the main Rutgers campus: Hegeman-234. It was tiny and dark, but it was his college dorm room! Ron and Todd helped move his belongings there a couple of days before classes began.

The next day, Phillip drove with Gillian and her mother to the University of Pennsylvania in downtown Philadelphia. After overseeing the move into Gillian's room, Mrs. Davis conveniently took a walk. Maybe, after all, she did remember how it was to be young and in love. Gillian and Phillip promised to call or write every chance they got. They made plans to get together in a week, since their campuses were only ninety minutes apart.

The end of summer brought feelings of joy and conflict to Brad. Business was terrific. The new catalogue was accepted even better than he had anticipated, and orders poured in by the ton. A rough calculation indicated that by the end of September, the previous year's gross would be surpassed—despite the recession!

Out of habit, Brad checked the new orders before they went to the processing area. Though the new computer system ran smoothly, he didn't trust it to tell him when supplies might run low at any given time.

" 'Scuse me, Boss."

"What's up, Tommy?"

"Gotta talk to you."

"What's on your mind?"

"I don't know how to say this. You've been so good to me and I appreciate everything you done for me."

"Tommy, cut the crap, what's wrong?"

"Nothing's wrong, except I gotta leave." Tommy held onto the edge of the desk. Brad bolted straight up.

"Where did this come from? Did I do something wrong because if I did, I apologize," Brad said. "Did you knock someone up, Tommy?"

"No, Boss," he said chuckling, "it's none of that. Ever since I was a kid, I wanted my own business. My wife's sister and her husband opened an auto center in Phoenix last month and can't handle the business. They asked me to come in with them. It's what I always wanted. What do you say, Boss?"

Brad shrugged. "Sounds great, Tommy. What can I say? I don't want to lose you."

"I was thinking I'd stay through November. That'll get you through the Christmas rush."

"You're not going to be easy to replace. Tommy?"

"Yeah, Boss?"

"I'm happy for you. As selfish as I want to be, you're doing the right thing. Good luck." Brad went to shake his hand but was knocked off balance by the manager's bear hug.

"Gee, Boss, I knew I could count on you. Well, got a lot to do. Thanks."

Brad returned to his desk and looked out his office window.

Brad and Trish learned to talk about what happened to her as a child. It was painful. They spent many emotionally draining nights discussing a lot of difficult feelings. As fearful as he was of losing a son, Brad realized how close he had come to losing his wife. They went for counseling, and he learned how to help her with her fears, her pain from childhood. And in doing so, he recognized that he, too, had protective walls surrounding him.

It was a beginning.

Labor Day weekend was quieter than usual in the Hunter household. Everyone felt Phillip's absence as he started Rutgers. Politicians and football players kicked off their fall campaigns but no one cared much until the winner-of-the-best-of seven-games was anointed at the World Series, proclaiming the true end of summer.

Children relished their last days of swimming and teachers prepared for their classes. New Broadway shows were ad-

219

vertised and old ones faded away. Days became shorter and nights were cooler. A crispness was in the air.

Fall was a crossroads—a season signifying change. Harvest moons and souls alike, it was a time for reaping and renewal.

❦❦

29

Even though it wasn't a fancy dinner, electricity filled the house. Ron and Todd knew to stay out of their mother's way. They helped when asked and hid at all other times. Brad ventured into the kitchen.

"You look nice," she said. Brad was wearing cobalt blue slacks and a matching print shirt.

"Thanks, so do you. Need help?"

"Fix me a drink. Everything's under control but I'm still nervous."

"Me, too." He went to the den and returned with two glasses filled to the brim. Taking hers, Trish thrust the glass toward Brad's.

"Cheers." They clinked as the doorbell rang.

They took hurried gulps and set them down, spilling some on the counter. Trish rushed toward the door, licking her fingers, and flung it open.

"I couldn't wait to see you. You look so great! So do you, Morris. C'mon in."

Classes had begun three weeks earlier and Brad and Trish had not seen Phillip since. Trish hugged him; he squirmed but she wouldn't let him go. After an interminable time, Phillip said, "Enough, Mom. I'll be here awhile."

"I know, but I missed you." She kissed him again. She turned to Brad. "Take them into the den. Dinner'll be ready in a few minutes."

Brad got Morris a drink.

"So? How do you like it, Phil?"

"School's great!"

"The students? The teachers? Tell me about them."

"Okay. Most of the students are from New Jersey. Since Rutgers joined the Big East, they've been recruiting big-time from the local jocks. We still get the farm boys from Ohio and Pennsylvania, but with Miami on the schedule, we're getting better. Classes aren't too hard yet, but there's more reading than I expected and you know how slow I am."

Brad turned to Morris. "And you? How are you doing?"

"Keeping busy. I had to see my lawyer a couple of times. I go to synagogue every day."

"With Esther gone, what're you doing with yourself?" Brad asked.

"Don't know. I can put more time into the shoe store on Route 18. They always need salesmen. It's no skin off their back, we work on commission."

"If you're serious about working more, how about. . . ."

The stove buzzer went off; Trish rang the cow bell.

"Dinner's ready. Phillip, get your brothers. They're probably playing Nintendo. Morris, you and Brad take a seat at the table." She floated into the kitchen, happy to have her family together, tipsy from the drink.

They took their places.

"Trish, do you have any honey?" Morris asked.

"I think so." She returned wiping the dust off a jar of Golden Blossom honey. On his second try, Morris got the cap to move; he dipped a spoon into the sticky honey and let some drip onto a piece of bread.

"This is for a sweet life, for good things, and good health."

"Amen, Morris. Let me have some of that," Brad said. He passed it around the table and everyone took theirs. Dinner began; it resembled the Oklahoma land rush. Trish hardly touched the food, preferring to sit back and watch the five men eat. In no time at all, nothing was left. The boys asked to be excused, leaving Brad, Trish, and Morris at the table.

"Dinner was delicious," Morris said. "Thank you."

"You're welcome." Trish looked at him. "Tell me, Morris, how are you *really* doing?"

"How am I supposed to be doing? I loved her very much. This is the first time we're separated in thirty years. She was part of me . . . but she's better off . . . the pain was too much."

"Phillip told me how. . . ."

"You people have been very nice to me. I have a lot to be thankful for," Morris said.

"Morris?" Trish reached for his hand. "Come with me." She led him to the couch, the same couch where Frank first looked at the photo album, where he told them about the hair sample and the blood test—where it all began.

Brad winked. She beamed back and cocked her head. She had never learned to wink and her awkward attempt always made him smile. He looked at the two of them. His wife sat tall, holding the hand of a man they had only met weeks earlier. Brad thought how strange life's twists and turns were, that no matter how you planned for it, fate had an agenda all its own.

"What is it, Trish?" Morris asked.

"Morris, tell me about Ari. Tell me about *our* son."

ABOUT THE AUTHOR

Alan A. Winter is a successful periodontist in New York City. A graduate of Rutgers University, he has taught periodontics at Columbia and New York University. He edited a dental periodical for many years, and has published articles in many distinguished professional journals.

Someone Else's Son is Winter's first novel; he is currently working on his second novel, as well as on a screenplay.

Additional copies of *Someone Else's Son* may be ordered by sending a check for $18.95 (please add the following for postage and handling: $2.00 for the first copy, $1.00 for each added copy) to:

MasterMedia Limited
17 East 89th Street
New York, NY 10128
(212) 260-5600
(800) 334-8232
(212) 546-7607 (fax)